Motown Monster

He She Black Widow II

Motown Monster

He She Black Widow II

by Leon Higgins

Senior Publisher
Steven Lawrence Hill Sr.

Awarded Publishing House
ASA Publishing Company

FOR MATURE READERS

Motown Monster

He She Black Widow II

by Leon Higgins

Senior Publisher
Steven Lawrence Hill Sr.

Awarded Publishing House
ASA Publishing Company

FOR MATURE READERS

ASA Publishing Company
An Accredited Publishing House with the BBB

105 E. Front St., Suite 101
Monroe, Michigan 48161
www.asapublishingcompany.com

Copyrights©2014, Leon Higgins, All Rights Reserved
Book: Motown Monster *He She Black Widow II*
Date Published: 3.10.2014
Edition 1 *Trade Paperback*
Book ASAPCID: 2380628
ISBN: 978-1-886528-66-6
Library of Congress Cataloging-in-Publication Data

This book was published in the United States of America.
State of Michigan

INTRODUCTION

Motown Monster is the sequel to the gutsy, raw, tell it like it is novel, . . . *He She Black Widow*

Tonya, at the age of seventeen, had been the girlfriend of the co-leader of a vicious dope dealing gang of juveniles in the city of Detroit.

With the face of a goddess and a body that looked as it had been carved from a mad sculptures dream. She had no problem using what she had to get what she wanted, and she soon became the unspoken power behind the gangs' underworld activities.

Having been raped by her uncle 'Gator' who was the leader of the Satan Disciples, a rival gang of the Diablo's, she had existed for one thing, and that was to get revenge against him. So she began her scheme of vindictiveness by making Rico, co-leader of the Diablo's fall in love with her. After getting him wrapped around her little finger, she sat out upon a plan to exact her revenge.

The first thing she had to do was to get rid of Jasper, whom was the leader of The Diablo's. This she was able to accomplish by instilling mistrust in Rico against Jasper, Her plan was to convince Rico that Jasper was only using him, and that Jasper was not really the smart one, but that he was really the brains behind the gang, and that Jasper was waiting for an opportunity to get rid of him. She knew that with Jasper out of the way, it would only be a matter of time before she got rid of Rico, and control of The Diablo's would be all hers.

Unknown to Rico or anybody else, Tonya was really in love with "Baldy" the co-leader of the Satan Disciples. With his help, they planned to get rid of 'Gator' and take control of the gang. If this could be accomplished it would be a piece of cake to unite both gangs under one rule . . . theirs.

But as with every good plan, nothing is foolproof, elements beyond Tonya's knowledge began to enter the picture and set off a chain of events that throws her plans into chaos. She had been counting on Rico getting killed in the plan that she and him had cooked up to get rid of Jasper, but things went wrong during the 'hit' and Rico escaped to come back home only to find 'Baldy' there with her. Surprised at this, Rico's suspicions turn to shock as Tonya and Baldy blurts out the whole sordid truth about how they had played him all the way, how they had lied and manipulated him into turning against Jasper, and how they had planned to take over the gangs with them at the seat of power.

But the most hurting revelation of all, was how she did not love him, but was in love with Baldy. Unable to stand hearing the truth, Rico and Baldy both reach for their guns, and as an eruption of deafening explosions sends the room into chaos, and then a uneasy calm, as both men lay dead.

After standing there looking at the dead men for what seemed like an eternity, reality floods over her. Accepting what had happened, realizing what she must do, she knows that there is nothing that she can do for her beloved 'Baldy'. So the only course of action left to her is to take the 'dope' and money and flee the carnage.

Teaming up with the rogue police officer; Sharon, they decide to escape the long arm of the law by fleeing to California. Along the way they encounter a series of events that sends the course of their lives on a roller coaster ride, a ride that turns them into the deadliest pair of assassins the world has ever known.

So get comfortable in your favorite easy chair . . . and prepare to meet the, **"Motown Monster"**.

Table of Contents

Motown Monster

He She Black Widow II

by Leon Higgins

Chapter 1

Reflections

Pulling the silk bed sheets up to cover her head and block out the bright sunlight, Tonya let out an exasperated moan as the alarm clock on the nightstand invades her sleep filled mind.

"Damn, not already. I just laid down."

Peeping one eye from under the covers, she takes a look at the clock to make sure it had the right time. There was no denying it, 8:00 a.m. time to get her ass in gear. Kicking the covers back, she stands up and stretches her arms over her head letting her voluptuous body extend to its full five feet, ten inch height. She feels a sense of comfort as her feet sinks deep into the snow-white plush carpet that covers the bedroom floor. The room is tastefully decorated in white and gold, at the center of which stands a gorgeous Italian styled King sized bed. On both sides of the white marble colored headboard, are twin nightstands of the same design.

Along one wall of the oversized room, there is a large dresser and along another wall is a wardrobe, all of the same décor.

Making her way into the adjoining master bathroom, which is decorated in white, trimmed with red accessories, she stands in front of the full length mirror that takes up one entire wall, and let her silk robe fall from her shoulders.

Staring at her image, she can't help to admire the sight of her magnificent body. Her breasts are full and erect with large marble-sized nipples. Her stomach is flat as a board and flares out into perfectly curved hips, hips that extend into a pair of long shapely, slightly bowed legs.

After admiring herself for a couple of minutes, she reaches into the shower and turns on the water, (wishing that she had enough time to take a bubble bath . . . but oh well!) After standing under the pulsating hot water for a few seconds, her pleasure is interrupted by the insistent ringing of the telephone.

"I don't believe this shit, can't a bitch wash her ass in peace?"

Storming from the shower with water dripping from her naked body, Tonya makes her way to the nightstand and blares into the phone.

"Who is it? And what the fuck you want?"

"Hey Tonya, it's me baby . . . Sharon! Who put a bug up your ass so early this morning?"

Recognizing the voice at the other end of the phone, Tonya's whole demeanor changes, lowering her voice to a purr, she answers, "Hi baby! You know I'm tickled to death to hear your voice, I can't tell you how much I've missed you. Come on up."

Hanging the house phone up, Sharon allows a smile to creep over her face as she heads for the elevator. She is resplendently dressed in a navy blue business suit with a powder blue ruffled shirt topped off with a dark blue necktie.

As she steps into the elevator, it amuses her to notice several men turning their heads to admire how the suit molds her body. After pushing the button on the elevator, she waits until it stops at the forty-second floor, she exit and walk toward a door marked Suite #426.

Upon knocking one time, the door is immediately opened and Sharon steps inside to be greeted by the naked

Tonya. Closing the door behind her; she is pulled into her waiting embrace. Allowing herself to be held close against her nakedness, Sharon can barely speak.

"Damn Baby, let a bitch breath, it ain't gon' do neither of us no good if you smother my ass to death," says a giggling Sharon.

"Sorry bout that love," snarls a kidding Tonya as she tries to fake a pout and attempted to push Sharon away from her. "I thought that just maybe you might be as glad to see me, as I am you. But look like I guessed wrong."

Not knowing if Tonya was serious or kidding, Sharon stops her giggling and pulls Tonya into her arms. Placing her lips against hers, she sucks greedily at her tongue until her legs grow weak from the ecstasy of it. Pushing Tonya back into the bedroom and onto the bed, she starts to run her hands slowly along her body. Abruptly sitting up and grabbing Sharon's hands, Tonya exclaims with shaky breath.

"Wait baby, wait a minute. Much as I want this, and you know I do. We ain't got time right now. When you called, I was just in the shower, matter of fact it's still running. Baby we got to go out to Century City for that meeting with Chavez."

"Okay, Love. I guess you're right. But remember, as soon as possible I'm going to feast on this big fine ass like it was a blue plate special, Now go on and finish your shower and get dressed."

Jumping up from the bed and heading for the bathroom, Tonya squeals with delight as Sharon bends over and kisses her on the cheek of her ass.

"Now stop that or I'll never get ready. Tell you what, why don't you get some of that oohh-weee out of the nightstand and roll us one while I finish getting ready?"

As Tonya goes into the bathroom, Sharon opens the nightstand drawer and takes out a plastic freezer bag, kicking her shoes off and settling back on the king size bed, she dumps some of the weed onto a piece of cardboard and separate the leaves from the stems and seeds. After expertly rolling two joints, she puts the bag back into the drawer and fires one of them up. Laying her head on the soft goose-down pillow, she takes a long drag on the joint and let the intoxicating smoke fill her lungs. As the strong weed began to take hold of her mind, she began to drift back into remembrance. Back to how it all started five years ago. She could see it as if it was just yesterday. It seems as if she was still sitting in the evidence room of the Detroit police department where she worked as a police officer. She remembers the empty feeling in the pit of her stomach as she read the memo that the dispatcher has placed in her hand. The memo informed her that there was going to be an audit and testing of all the confiscated drugs that was being held in the department's evidence room . . . the evidence room that she was in charge of.

She had been a seasoned cop in the Detroit police department, and a good one at that . . . up until she fell head over heels in love with Detective Samuel Simmons . . . who just happened to be the main drug supplier to a Detroit street gang. Realizing the value of Sharon's position, Simmons wasted no time using Sharon's weakness for him to his advantage, it wasn't long before he had her working with him in his drug business. Sharon would steal the confiscated drugs and substitute them with flour. Then Simmons would sell the dope to the gang and they would share in the profit, it was a foolproof plan, not only was she making a shit-load of money, but it also gave her an opportunity to be close to him. The plan was working great and she wasn't worried about the scheme being discovered because she was in charge of the drugs. She knew that when any particular trial was over, whatever drugs were connected to it would be destroyed and nobody would be the wiser that they would only be destroying flour.

This could have gone on forever except for one thing . . . something just wasn't right. Something about Simmons had her puzzled. She knew that she was good looking, with a killer body. But no matter what she did, she just couldn't get Simmons to screw her.

His excuse had been that even though he was crazy about her, he didn't believe in mixing business with pleasure . . . especially with the kind of job they had. Being a cop was dangerous enough without having to worry about somebody that you are involved with, being exposed to the same dangers everyday. No, he just couldn't put her through that.

Well, that may have worked up until that night when she had been visiting Simmons apartment, upon leaving, she had forgot her purse and had to go back unannounced to retrieve it. Approaching the slightly ajar apartment door, she heard sounds coming from inside. Peeping through the crack, her heart skipped a beat and stood still. She couldn't believe what she was seeing. There was a man standing with his back to her with his pants down around his ankles. But what took her breath away was the sight of Detective Simmons on his knees with the man's dick in his mouth.

As Simmons caught sight of her, he could only stare stupidly at her. The man, upon hearing the commotion, pulled his dick out of Simmons mouth, pulled his pants up and ran from the apartment.

Sharon stepped into the apartment as a flood of emotions swept through her. Now she understood why Simmons wasn't sexually interested in her, now she understood that all she meant to him was a way to get his dope, while playing her and making her believe his lines of bull shit about looking out for her welfare.

As the hurt gave way to anger, the only thing she had in mind at this time was MURDER. She charged at him before he could get up off the floor and dished out one hell of a government Grade-A ass whipping. The more she whipped on that ass, the madder she got.

"And to think nigga, I thought something was wrong with me, and all the time it was because you were a stinking dick sucking fag." She screamed as she continued the assault on Simmons until he passed out.

After that, her association with Simmons and their dope deal was over. He had tried to persuade her to continue on the business end, but she wasn't having it, she didn't want anything to do with him or the drugs.

During this venerable time in her life, she met Tonya. Tonya knew that Sharon was the main source of Simmons drug supply, and when she found out what went down between them, she knew it was a golden opportunity for her to convert Sharon to her team. After calling her and informing her that she knew what had been going down with her and Simmons, she got Sharon to agree to meet her.

Being a cop, Sharon made sure that she was prepared for whatever bullshit Tonya might have up her sleeve . . . after all it seemed as if Tonya knew all about her and her involvement with Simmons, but she didn't know jack-shit about her, and it made her mighty nervous for somebody to have that kind of edge on her.

The first thing that she did was to get Tonya to meet her at a place of her choosing . . . and she made sure that that place was somewhere that they wasn't going to be seen together, or that the place wasn't bugged. After all, she was still a cop, and she didn't know if Tonya was working undercover in a sting operation for internal affairs or if she was on the up and up. The safest place that she could think of was her own home, so that's where she told her to come.

After Tonya arrived at Sharon's home and rung the door bell, Sharon peeped through the peephole to make sure that she was alone, satisfied that she was by herself, Sharon opened the door just wide enough for her to squeeze in.

Pointing her service 9mm at her, Sharon hisses in a low deadly voice.

"Okay Bitch, what's your game? You have about two seconds to state your business before I make you wish you had never heard of me, and the clock is ticking."

Staring down the muzzle of the nine-millimeter, Tonya is at a loss for words.

"Whoa there lady, take it easy," says Tonya in a not too sure voice. "I told you on the phone, I just want to talk business."

"And what kind of business do you think you have with me?"

"Like I told you on the phone, I know all about what you and Detective Simmons had going on, and I know about what happened out to his crib," blurts Tonya excitedly as she detects that she is losing her edge with Sharon.

"Hold on bitch, before you say another word, who sent you?" says Sharon with her voice growing more deadly. Pulling the hammer back on the nine, she aims the muzzle at Tonya's forehead. "Your two seconds are up, so your answer had better be to my liking."

Tonya can feel her bladder about to give way as she feel the coldness of the steel pressed against her head. But she knows that this is her one and only chance. Not only to make a deal with Sharon for the drugs, but also to get her ass out of here in one piece. Summoning up courage that she did not feel, she slowly raises her hand and gently pushes the gun aside.

"Look Ho! I didn't come here for this bullshit," says Tonya, trying hard as she can to keep her knees from knocking. "I brought my black ass over here in good faith cause I thought you be a fo real bitch and be interested in making some money. Now here you come with this off the wall bullshit fo you even hear me out, well, I got better things to do with my time. . . I'm otta here."

"Not so fast sister, I'm the one that's holding the gun so I'm the one that's calling the shots. How do I know you're not internal affairs . . . maybe even the Feds? I don't know shit about you."

Having gone too far to turn around, Tonya jumps right to the offense. Raising her voice she stammers.

"Bitch is you crazy? Internal affairs . . . whatever the fuck that is . . . or the Feds, Look I'm a dope dealer. I sell drugs, nothing more, nothing less. I told you, I came over here to try to make a deal with you to buy some of that bomb-ass dope that you and Simmons was getting ya'll hands on . . . that's all."

Stepping back a few feet, Sharon still has the gun trained on her. With her voice lightening up a little, she replies.

"That's what you say, But how do I know that you are not wired?"

"Wired . . . bitch, you ARE crazy," spits Tonya, with more courage creeping into her voice. "So you think I'm wired huh . . . watch this." Stepping back a few feet from Sharon, Tonya began to undue the buttons on her blouse. After letting it slide to the floor, she reaches behind her back and unfasten her bra. As the lace material releases its twin hostages, her breast spring straight out in an erect posture. Moving her hands down to the snaps on the skintight jeans that she is wearing, she unsnaps them and peels them down . . . panties and all, in one motion.

At the sight of her standing there naked to the world, Sharon is surprised at the sudden display. Unable to tear her gaze away from Tonya's body, she is also surprised that her breathing has become a little raspy as she thinks to herself.

"Man, this bitch has a body on her."

"Have you seen enough? Are you satisfied that I ain't wearing no goddam wire? I told you what I'm here fo, strictly business. Now if I can pull my draws back up, maybe we can talk?"

Sharon could only nod her head dumbly up and down. She had a strange reluctance to watch Tonya pull her clothes up and deny her the privilege of seeing her voluptuous body any longer.

Sharon's interest in her body had not gone unnoticed by Tonya as she made a mental note to herself on how she could use that to her advantage at a latter time. As she slowly pulled her panties up her legs, she made exaggerated moves to position them into place.

Next she made sure she wiggled and squirmed as she pulled her pants up and stuffed her ass inside of them. Then she replaced her blouse . . . not bothering to put her bra back on, which she stuffed into her pocket. She purposely left the top buttons unfastened to show her cleavage. With no bra on, her nipples were very visible as they strained against the fabric of the blouse.

After Tonya has finished dressing, she has to call Sharon's name several times to get her attention.

"I said can we talk?" shouts Tonya.

"Huh? What did you say? Yea! Yea, I guess we can." Says a embarrassed Sharon as her mind is snapped back to the situation at hand.

Wondering if Tonya had paid attention to her awkward moment, in a nervous voice she instructs her to have a seat.

Walking across the highly polished hardwood floor, the heels of Tonya's boots make a tap, tap, tap sound as she takes a seat on the comfortable black leather sofa. Regaining her composure, Sharon sticks her nine-millimeter into the holster on her hip and takes a seat beside her.

"Okay, so you've convinced me that you're not wearing a wire. But that don't mean that you're not undercover."

"Look, I'll tell you what!" says Tonya feeling more at ease and pleased at the way things are going. Reaching into her pants pocket, she pulls out a 'joint'. "Now you being a cop and all, I know you know about entrapment."

Taking a lighter from the same pocket, she fires it up. Sucking the acrid smoke into her lungs, she says between clenched teeth. "I've been in enough courtrooms to know how that shit works. They say that if the police initiate an unlawful act and persuade somebody to participate in it, then that's entrapment and anything associated with that arrest is illegal. Am I right?"

Eyeing her with a quizzical look on her face, Sharon speaks.

"I know the law, what's your point?"

Passing the weed to her, Tonya replies. "My point is this. I'm smoking this 'joint', and I'm encouraging you to hit it with me. Now unless the law don' changed, possession of weed is still illegal, so if I be a cop and be encouraging you to break the law then anything that comes from this wouldn't be admissible in court, right?"

Amazed at her knowledge of the law, Sharon thinks for a minute. Eyeing her with renewed suspicion, she asks, "If you're not a cop, how do you know so much about how the law works?"

At this point, Tonya's confidence is growing by leaps and bounds. So with a bit of bragging in her voice, she replies.

"Like I told you, I don been in enough courtrooms with friends of mine to see how that shit works. So here, go ahead and take a pull on this gangster weed and let's get down to business."

After staring at the offered 'joint' for what seemed an eternity, for reasons that she couldn't understand, Sharon finds herself accepting it. There was something about this girl that seemed to put her at ease and she couldn't understand the magnetic attraction that was slowly sweeping through her.

Taking a long pull on it, she allowed the powerful drug to invade her brain and put her even more at ease. After giving the weed a few minutes to do its work, Sharon begin to speak in a mellow tone, "Just say for the sake of argument that I do believe you . . . and I'm not saying that I do, but if you are coming at me straight, what do you want with me?"

"I'm gon' come right out with the fo' real," says a beaming Tonya as she realizes that she has Sharon right where she wants her. "Like I told you, I know all about the thing you and Simmons had going on and I know what happened. Now my guess is now that yawls little romance is over, you be needing a new business partner. Now the Diablo's still be needing a connect fo' our drugs, so with Simmons not being in the picture, you can deal directly with me."

"Whoa there little lady," says Sharon as the sounds of Tonya's incriminating words clears the influencing weed from her mind. "First of all I'm going to do a very through check on you, and if anything shitty comes up in your background, you're going to wish to hell that you had never tried to run this shit on me. And another thing, even if you are straight, what makes you think that I'm looking for another partner?"

"Sharon, baby, use your head. Detective Simmons was dealing with the Diablo's because he knew we could move all the shit he could supply us with . . . but you supplied him. So with you and him not being cool no mo', that puts you in the driver's seat. And believe me, ain't nobody gon' move the kind of weight that we can."

With a sudden look of sadness coming over her face, Sharon speaks in a muffed voice, "Let me tell you something that you probably don't understand about me and Simmons relationship. The reason that I got involved in this shit with him in the first place, was not for the money, but because I loved the mutha-fucka. But after I found out that he was a low life dick-sucking bastard, that shit is over. So what makes you think that I still want any part of any of that shit anymore?"

Seeing the tear that is about to well up in Sharon's eye, Tonya puts her arm around her waist and allows her head to rest on her shoulder.

"Now, Now," whispers Tonya in soft soothing voice, "Being a woman, I can understand how men can fuck up a wet dream, but that's where you have to learn how to think fo' yourself, Don't let a man be the only thing in yo' life that means anything to you. Look, Simmons disappointed you but don't let that stop you from making yo' paper. Girl you better stop and think."

Lying against Tonya's body, Sharon becomes aware of Tonya's bra-less nipples pressing against breast. Strange she thought.

"Why in the hell is this girl affecting me like this?" She couldn't understand it; all she knew was that it was the most heavenly feeling she had ever experienced. Reluctantly she pushes herself away from her body and with labored breath, makes a declaration.

"Whew . . . I think we've talked enough for today, but I'll tell you what . . . like I said, I'm going to check you out and we'll see where this is going okay?" Realizing what effect she's is having on her, Tonya does the unexpected. Reaching over, she pulls Sharon's head toward her and before Sharon realizes what is happening, Tonya sticks her tongue into her mouth and slowly works it down her throat. And as if her lips had a life of their own, and against her will, she finds herself hungrily sucking on the offering.

Thrill after thrill pulsates through her surprised body until something snaps her back to reality. Extracting herself from Tonya's embrace, she shouts, "What the fuck do you think you're doing bitch? What the fuck do you think I am . . . some kind of dyke or something? I think you had better leave and I do mean now!"

Reaching into her purse, Tonya takes a card with her name and phone number on it and holds it out to Sharon.

"Here, when you be ready to talk, call me."

Walking out of the house, she has a satisfied smile on her face.

"Now I know just how to work her fine ass, and believe me I'm going to work her over time.

"Standing at the door with the card in her hand, Sharon can only stare dumbly at it and wonder what in the hell just happened.

For the next few days, try as she might, Sharon could not get Tonya off her mind. Every time she relived the scene of Tonya embracing her and sliding her tongue down her throat, her legs would go weak.

"What the hell is wrong with me? Here I am a grown ass woman, and all that I can think about is another woman! I've got to stop this shit and get myself together."

But as the days passed by, she discovered that that was easier said than done. Up until she had meet Tonya, she had never entertained the thought of anything close to an intimate feeling towards another female, so what was it about this girl that she couldn't stop thinking of her, But she did know one thing . . . if she didn't find out, she was going to go crazy.

The insistent ringing of Tonya's phone awakens her from a light sleep. Reaching over to retrieve it from the floor where it had dropped while she had fallen asleep on the sofa watching T.V. she mumbles, "Yeah . . . who is it?"

"Hello, can I speak to Tonya?"

"This is Tonya, who's calling?"

"This is Sharon!" comes a half apologetic voice, "But if you're asleep I can call back later."

Hearing Sharon's voice on the phone, Tonya's mind immediately becomes crystal clear.

"Oh no, no, no, Ain't no problem. I'm woke, I was just watching a little T.V. and I must've dozed off. But nah, I'm woke now. What's up?"

Now that she had made the call, Sharon began to feel a little uneasy about the whole thing, she had practiced a thousand times what she was going to say, but now that she had actually did it, she had a hard time getting the right words to come out.

"Ummm, listen Tonya. I aaahh, I aahh, I did that checking that I told you I was going to do. Yeah, well everything checked out right, so I guess you are coming for real. So listen, if you still want to talk? I guess we can."

"Hey, now that's what I'm talking bout," comes Tonya's excited voice.

"Now you talking, and I promise you that you won't be sorry. So you just tell me when and where."

Hearing the excitement in Tonya's voice, sets off a delicious feeling in her.

"Well if you're not doing anything, what about now?" asks Sharon, surprised at her own anxiousness.

"No, I'm not doing a thing. Tell you what . . . give me enough time to shower, and I'll be right over. Is that all right?"

"That will be fine, I'll see you when you get here."

After hanging up the phone, Tonya thinks to herself.

"I knew it, I knew that bitch would call. I know I read that bitch right the first time. She might wanna do business true enough . . . but she be interested in another kind of business too. . . Monkey business . . . my monkey! She might not know it yet, but she's a undercover pussy licker and I'm just the right bitch to help her discover everything that she needs to know about what a real woman can do fo' her."

After taking her shower, Tonya sprinkles on her most provocative perfume and selects her most sexy underwear. Dressing in a to-die-for cream color low-rider pants suit, she smiles to herself.

"Time fo' mama to go to work."

Chapter 2

The turning point

Hearing the knock; knock; knock on her door, Sharon is nervous as a cat as she goes to answer it. Seeing Tonya standing there looking like a virtual goddess, it takes everything she has to keep her composure. Trying to remain all business, she smiles politely, "Hi Tonya, come on in and have a seat."

With Tonya walking ahead of her towards the sofa, Sharon's heart skips a beat. Try as she may, she can't take her eyes away from the seesawing motion that Tonya's ass is making inside of the skintight pants that she is wearing. Taking a seat on the sofa besides her, Sharon calmly starts.

"Okay Tonya, like I said over the phone. I checked you out and you came up clean. I'm true to my word . . . I said I would talk to you so here I am, go ahead." Tonya says to herself.

"Okay Miss Thang, if that's the way you want to play it, all righty then. I'll play yo' little game. First of all Sharon, I want to thank you fo' letting me come back over here after the way I acted the last time. I just don't know what came over me. I 'pologize fo' that."

Caught off guard at her mentioning the kiss, Sharon blushes and manages to stammer.

"Yes, yes of course I accept your apology."

"Good, that's great cause I sho' don't wanna do anything to fuck up our partnership." Says a smiling Tonya as she thinks to herself. "This ho' wants me bad . . . I can see it in her eyes, don't worry baby, befo' I leave, you gon' git everything you want and then some."

"Wait a minute Tonya, about this partnership thing. I told you why I did that with Simmons, it wasn't just for the money, it was mostly for him. Now, ahhh, I just don't know!" Tonya thinks to herself.

"This dizzy ass mutha-fucka gon' play this shit out to the very end. Well if that's the way she wants to play the GAME, it's time to show her I invented the mutha-fuckin' RULES, it's time to take the kid gloves off. All right Sharon, I can understand where you be coming from and I can respect that, so I'm not gon' beat a dead horse! But just let me say this befo' I go. You say you didn't do it fo' the cheese? Hey, that's great, but I don't care how much money you got, I don't know nobody that's got so much that they can't use a little mo', but if you be the first one, then congratulations.

When I came over here the other day, yeah, it was all about business, but when I started to talk to you something happened. I just got through 'pologizing fo' kissing you . . . well FUCK THAT! . . . I take that back, I ain't 'pologizing fo' shit; I did it because I wanted to and it felt damn good. Now you can bull shit yo' self all you want, But I know you felt it too, I know you want me just as much as I want you and I had hoped that we could be mo' than just business partners, but I see that I was wrong. But anyway, thank you fo' yo' time."

Getting off the sofa, Tonya heads towards the door making sure she swings her hips in her sexiest walk. Reaching the door she pauses for an instant and turns toward Sharon who is still sitting on the sofa totally confused at what she has just heard. "Sharon befo' I go let me ask you one thing, will you do me a favor? If it don't mean nothing to you then it won't matter. Will you let me kiss you befo' I go?"

Startled, Sharon is at a loss for words.

"I, I, I, don't know what you mean! Why are you talking to me like this? I, I, I don't know what to say!"

Walking back to the sofa, Tonya sits beside her. "Sharon . . . Sharon listen to me! First of all you can stop bull shitting yo' self. I guarantee you that yo' draws are as wet as mine, only I'm woman enough to admit it. And you would too if you would just trust in yo' feelings and let yo' self go."

Once again, before Sharon can react, Tonya pulls her head to her and presses her lips to hers, only this time as their lips meet, its Sharon who darts her tongue inside of Tonya's mouth. After embracing in a kiss that seemed to go on for hours, Sharon breaks free and stammer in a shaky voice.

"Tonya, you have to understand. I've never been with a woman before. I, I, I wouldn't know what to do."

With her voice lowering almost to a whisper, she admits, "Yes, yes you're right, Oh god Tonya, you're right, I want you so bad I can't stand it, but baby I just don't know what to do."

"Schuush," whispers a beaming Tonya as she pulls Sharon back into her arms. "Don't worry my love, I'll show you everything that you need to know. You've already taken the first step, now we can go the rest of the way together."

Standing up from the sofa, Tonya reaches out to Sharon. As if she is in a fog, she accepts the out stretched hand and follows her into the bedroom. The bedroom is decorated in various shades of pink with a comfortable queen sized bed taking up half of the room.

Sitting on the bed, Tonya instructs Sharon to turn on the lights.

A little perplexed, she asks, "Why? Why do you want the lights on?"

In a soothing but slightly stern voice, Tonya replies.

"Just do it baby, I've got my reasons, just trust me."

After turning the lights on, Sharon starts back towards the bed.

"Stop right there," Whispers Tonya. "Stop right where you are."

Surprised at her unexpected orders, Sharon wonders what is going on.

"Why don't you want me to come over there with you?"

"Because all I want you to do right now, is what I tell you to do," says Tonya, putting a little authority in her voice.

"And the first thing I want you to do is take yo' sweater off and let it drop to the flo."

After being a cop for so long, Sharon feels a little uneasy about someone not in a position of authority giving her orders, but never the less she finds herself obeying. Raising the sweater over her head, she lets it drop to the floor.

"Good, good . . . that's my sweet little bitch," coos Tonya. Now do the same with the bra."

As per instructions, Sharon follows orders. After the bra drops, and her succulent breast pops in to view, she feels a little ashamed that her nipples are starting to harden. Timidly she stands there facing Tonya with her hands trying to cover her tits.

"Baby, I'm getting a little embarrassed, do we have to do it like this?"

"Like I said sweetheart, just trust me," says a delighted Tonya at Sharon's discomfort. All the while getting a little annoyed at herself for not being able to completely control the feeling of sexual arousal that is beginning to flow through her body. But determined to suppress it, she maintains control as she thinks to herself, 'It didn't have to be like this, but you be the one that wanted to bull shit and play games. Well welcome to my world Ho'. I'm in charge now . . . "I want you to very slowly unfasten yo' jeans and pull them down, not off .

. . just down as far as you can get them. And then I want you to do the same with yo' panties."

After complying with Tonya's orders, Sharon, began to experience a strange sensation. Standing there with her body totally exposed, her embarrassment began to turn to excitement.

"Okay, now bring yo fine ass over here to me," teases Tonya.

Hobbling over to the bed with her clothes around her ankles, Sharon stands before Tonya who is still seated.

"What do you want me to do now your majesty?" asks Sharon, warming to the game.

"I want you to put your hands behind your back and stand perfectly still."

Getting off the bed, Tonya goes behind Sharon and began to gently blow on the back of her neck. With nothing but her cool breath touching her body, she began to slowly blow back and forth across her back creating tiny goose bumps as she goes. As she continues to blow, she moves the air stream down her body and between the cheeks of her ass, where she makes slow circling motions. With the soothing air currents massaging her body, Sharon is unaware of the low moans that are beginning to come from her own throat.

Instructing her to turn around, Tonya repeats the same procedure on the front of her body. Starting with her breast, she gently blows the cool air across her nipples causing them to harden even more.

With the cool air causing a tingling sensation in her body, Sharon instinctively reaches out to grab at Tonya's head, only to be rebuffed.

"I told you to stand still, didn't I," reprimanded Tonya. "If I have to tell you again, I'm going to stop. Is that what you want me to do?"

Afraid that she would take away the delicious feeling, Sharon pleaded.

"No please don't stop. Please, I'll do whatever you say, just don't stop."

With the satisfaction of knowing that she was in full control, Tonya continued with her work. Renewing her assault, she trails the cool air down across Sharon's stomach until she comes into contact with the bushy patch of hair that is nestled between her legs.

Gently blowing the hair aside, Tonya concentrates the air stream to her clit, which causes Sharon to moan with ecstasy.

"Okay now," barks Tonya, "now that she is satisfied that Sharon is fully aroused. Take yo' clothes all the way off and lay down."

A little miffed at Tonya for stopping the air massage that she had been receiving, Sharon hurriedly obeys and takes her clothes off, anxious to find out what else she has in store for her.

With Sharon lying on the bed, Tonya began to take off her own clothes. When she is finally naked, Sharon greedily reaches for her, but is instantly admonished.

"What the hell do you think you be doing?" barks Tonya.

Puzzled, Sharon asks, "What do you mean? I just want to touch you."

"You just want to touch me . . . did I ask you to touch me? I told you, all I want you to do is what I tell you. Now can you do that or do we stop right now?"

Not knowing why Tonya is becoming so angry, Sharon fears that she would stop now and deny her the most intoxicating feeling that she had ever experienced. To prevent this, she submits herself fully.

"I'm so sorry Tonya, whatever you say, I'll do. Just please don't stop," says Sharon in a submissive voice.

"That's better," beams the triumphant Tonya.

"That's much better, I'm going to say this fo' the last time, if you make one move without my permission, I'll stop and no second chance, understand?"

Passively, Sharon nods her head up and down.

"Wonderful, now that we understand each other, here's what I want you to do. Reach down and give me yo' panties off the flo.'"

Not daring to risk angering her with questions, Sharon immediately obeys.

Taking the panties from her, Tonya instructs Sharon to raise her arms above her head while she uses them to tie her hands together. Next she takes her own discarded panties and pulls them over Sharon's head, blinding her except for the small amount of light that seeps through the thin material. With the feminine aroma of Tonya's panties assaulting her nose, Sharon's heart begin to beat like a trip-hammer. And her sexual arousal is heightened by the fact that she can't see what is going on.

Bending over her body with nothing touching her but the tongue, Tonya starts a slow deliberate journey down Sharon's body. Starting first at the neck with a light delicate licking motion, she trails the wet kisses down to her tits and the rock hard nipples. Taking the nipples between her teeth, she gently massages them with her tongue as Sharon's body began to twitch and her breath starts to come in short gasps.

After sucking on her tits for what seemed like hours, she moves her tongue down to her navel where she darts it inside and gently sucks away before moving down to her thigh. Gently nipping at the flesh with her teeth, she alternates between nipping and sucking. Licking her tongue up and down her thigh, coming close to her pussy with the intension of invading it only to move the tongue away at the last moment.

With the exquisite sensations running through her body, Sharon is about to go out of her mind. She desperately wants to reach down and guide Sharon's head to her pussy, a pussy that is burning from neglect of a tongue that is so near but so far away. But she don't dare, she remembers the warning, she knows that if she removes her hands from over her head, Tonya might stop what she's doing and she would be goddam if she would risk that.

"Aaahhhh, Aaaaaa," came the tortured sounds emanating from Sharon's throat as Tonya expertly administered a tongue whipping on her. Just as she thought that she would make it through this alive, Tonya switched her assault methods. Taking her hands, she gently pulled the lips of her pussy open and exposed the pea-sized clit. Taking it between her lips, she rapidly moved her tongue back and forth over it. Feeling the contact, Sharon let out a long death-defying scream and beyond all control, she grabbed Sharon's head and tried to stuff it inside of her. Not bothering to move her hands from her head, Tonya stabs her tongue deep inside of the pussy. Taking Sharon's legs and placing them on each side of her head, Tonya begins her assault in earnest. Reaching beneath Sharon's ass with both her hands, she pulls her tight against her mouth and starts to rapidly drive her tongue in and out of Sharon's wet pussy, she continues until she hears the animalistic sounds coming from Sharon's throat.

"AAAAhhhhh, oh my god, you're killing me, help me pleeeeeease, Ahhhhhhhh." Sharon screams at the top of her voice as her body twitches and bucks under the assault of Tonya's tongue. She feels the storm starting from the bottom of her feet and intensifies as it travels up her body to explode between her legs. "Ooooooooohhhhhh my godddddddddddd," she let out one loud blood curdling scream and faints dead away.

Chapter 3

Dangerous Decisions

After that night which now seemed so long ago, Sharon's mind was centered on one thing and one thing only . . . Tonya. She had agreed to become Tonya's new partner in the drug business . . . Hell, after what Tonya had whipped on her, she would have confessed to the sinking of the Titanic if she had asked her too. She knew that she was hopelessly in love with her and it felt great. But just as they were getting things in order, the shit hit the fan.

First came that thing about Detective Simmons getting killed by what everybody thought was a man, but turned out to be a psychopathic woman masquerading as one. She didn't have any remorse what so ever about hearing how he met his end.

"Good riddance to that faggot brother-fucker," she thought. "He could have had all this" . . . indicating herself . . . "But he chose to chase the dick, well, I'm glad he found what he was looking for."

But what she didn't know was that Tonya, through her conniving and scheming, had set off a chain of events that was about to blow their whole drug empire to bits. She didn't know that Tonya had started a blood bath between the two deadliest gangs in Detroit and that she was about to get burned. With the wholesale killings and wide-open drug trafficking that was taking place, The D.E.A. had become involved in the Detroit Police Department and they were not leaving any stone unturned. In their investigation, some questions surfaced about the department's confiscated drugs, and ordered an audit. With Sharon being in charge of the evidence room, she knew that with any kind of audit, that meant one thing . . . her ass! Well she was a firm believer in the old saying . . . "Catching comes before killing," and she damn sure wasn't about to stay around and be caught.

While sitting around trying to figure out what would be her best move, her thoughts were interrupted by the ringing of her cell phone. It was Tonya, she briefly told her what had went down at Rico's house and informed her that she was leaving town right now.

"Wait a minute Tonya, blurted Sharon in a loud whisper. I'm so glad you called baby, I'm in a world of trouble. I have to talk to you, but not over the phone. I need to meet you right away, where are you?"

"I'm 'bout to hit I-94 and get the hell out of dodge. I told you I got to go, I'll call you when I get to wherever I'm going. Right now I don't know where that's going to be."

"Tonya! Tonya!" hollers Sharon trying not to scream. "Listen to me baby. I haven't got time to explain over the phone, but the shit has hit the fan and I've got to get out of here. Now tell me where you are."

Hearing the edge in Sharon's voice, Tonya tries to think. "All right, all right. Let me think fo a minute. Okay tell you what. You know where the foot of the Boulevard and Jefferson is? You be there in thirty minutes, thirty minutes no mo'. If you ain't there I'm gon'. I swear it Sharon, after thirty minutes I'm gon'."

"Thirty minutes, okay I'm on my way," replies Sharon as she scurries about the evidence room grabbing her coat and purse. Locking up the room after her, she takes the elevator to the main floor of police headquarters and dashes out of a back door and makes a beeline for her car.

Thankful that she hadn't encountered any of her fellow officers, she leaves the parking lot and drives toward the rendezvous spot. It was all she could do to keep her speed at the legal limit, because she sure didn't want to attract any unwanted attention. Glancing at the clock on her dashboard she knew her time was almost up.

"Damn it, she can't be gone, she has to still be there!"

Just as she was approaching the parking lot, a car was pulling out ahead of her. Recognizing that the driver was Tonya, she started franticly blowing on her horn. Looking through her rear view mirror, Tonya notices her and pulls over. Coming to a stop behind her, Sharon jumps out of her car and opening the door of Tonya's, she gets in and grabs her in a bear hug embrace.

"Oh my god baby, man, I'm so glad I got here in time, I don't know what I would have done if I had missed you," says an excited Sharon as the words poured out her mouth.

Feeling a wave of tenderness wash over her, Tonya purrs. "Hey love. I'm glad you got here too, but this ain't the end of the world. I told you I was gon' call you as soon as I got to where I was going, and I meant it. Now what so important that you made me wait?" ask Tonya with a little irritation creeping into her voice.

Just the sensation of being close to her body, gave Sharon strength. After telling Tonya all about what was going on at police headquarters, she seemed to run out of breath as she just sat there in silence.

"God dam!" says Tonya letting out a long whistle and putting both of her hands up to her head. Now I see why you be in a hurry. What you plan on doing?"

"I don't know, I was hoping that you would have something in mind."

"Something in mind, something in mind like what? I told you what went down at Rico's house and I ain't waiting fo' the cops to put two and two together and hang my black ass. I'm getting the fuck otta here."

With a touch of fear at facing this alone creeping into her voice, Sharon finds herself on the verge of tears.

"Baby, that's the answer. You have to get away from here and so do I." says Sharon with a shaky voice. "That's the solution; we can go together. Don't you see? It's perfect, we can look out for each other."

Thinking about it for a moment, Tonya sees the advantage in what Sharon is saying.

"After all," she thinks to herself. "If you be running from the cops, who better to have with you than a cop that can tell you how they think."

"Sharon, you right baby. Yeah, we can do this shit together but we got to leave right now, we ain't got time to fuck around."

"Yes," she cries as she plants kisses all over Tonya's face. And I promise you. You won't be disappointed. All I have to do is go home and pack a few things."

"Bitch is you insane?" shouts Tonya. "Our black asses be 'bout as hot as a fire cracker on the fourth of July, and you want to go home and pack; pack my ass, we got to get the fuck otta here, that's what we gotta do, and I mean right now while the getting is good."

"But what about my car? What about my clothes? What about my house?"

"What 'bout all that shit? You better start thinking what 'bout yo' black ass! Listen, fo' all intents and purposes you ain't no cop no mo' . . . you be wanted by them now, you be on the other side so you better start thinking like one, that's the only way we gon' get out of this shit. So help me figure out how we gon' do this."

As Tonya's words sink into her mind, the reality of the situation finally hits home. Storing away the childish emotions that she had just a moment ago, her professional training and intellect takes over.

"Yeah baby you're right. I don't know what came over me but I'm all right now. Let's see, after the D.E.A. does their audit tomorrow, they're going to be combing every bush looking for my ass, so that gives me a little time. I went shopping yesterday and I never took my clothes out of my trunk, that gives me a couple of outfits to wear. So the first thing that I need to do is get out of this uniform and into some civvies."

"Okay so get yo' shit and lets git otta here, you can leave yo' car right here."

"No, no that would give the police a reference point to start looking for me. You said that I should start thinking like a cop; well that's what I'm doing. Like I said, there're not going to start looking for me until tomorrow so we have a little time to do some things. The first thing that I want you to do is follow me out to Metro. Airport."

"Metro airport?" asks Tonya with a quizzical look on her face. "What the fuck we gon' do out there?"

"We are going to give them a false lead and buy us some time. When they find my car out there, they're going to figure that I left town by plane, and by the time they check all of the flight manifest for all the planes that have left between today and tomorrow, we'll be long gone and they won't know which way we went."

With a smile creeping over her face, Tonya agrees.

"I knowed you be one smart bitch, that's my baby! Come on, let's get going."

"Not so fast, slow down babygirl, like I said, we have a little time to think this thing through," caution's Sharon as her police training kicks into high gear. "Do you have any money?"

"What do you mean? Why do you ask that? Tonya asks suspiciously.

"Look Tonya, before we go any farther with this I think we had better get on the same page. This is not a game that we're about to play." Barks Sharon, surprised at the authoritarian voice than she is speaking in. "This shit is for real. If the police catch up with me, I know what that means, life in prison . . . and I'm damn sure going to do everything in my power to make sure that that doesn't happen. And you have even more to lose than I do, think about it, with your fingerprints all over that house, how long do you think it's going to take the police to start looking for you? Baby we're talking about murder. And another thing, judging by what you said went down, you didn't mention it, But it's my guess that with you being the only one left alive, there has to be a awful lot of dope and money somewhere and I just can't imagining you walking away and leaving it there, and with Jasper still out there somewhere, you know he's going to be looking for your sweet ass. So you see, both of our asses are in deep shit and the only chance that we have is to trust each other."

Digesting what Sharon has just said, Tonya has to agree that she is making sense.

"Yeah, you right . . . yeah I got the cheese and dope, but what 'bout you! You got any?"

"Yes," Admits Sharon. "I have about two hundred thousand, but it's deposited in off shore accounts. I couldn't afford to have that kind of money in a regular bank account because it would raise too many questions . . . where would a cop get that kind of money? I have the pass codes tucked safely away in a safe deposit box." Glancing at her watch, she states. "The bank closes in about an hour, so that gives me plenty of time to get there. In the meantime, here's what I want you to do. Go out to the airport and wait at the arrival gate. When I get there, I'll go in the departure terminal and walk around before I come down there to meet you."

"Why you want to do that? Somebody might see you."

"That's what I'm counting on . . . I want somebody to remember seeing me there when the police come looking for me. Like I said, I want them to think that I left by plane."

"Damn baby, that be some slick shit, with you and me together we can't lose," grins Tonya excitedly.

"Like I said, as long as we're straight with each other, we have a chance." Reaching over and giving Tonya a long kiss, Sharon teases, "Now get your fine ass out of here and take care of business, I'll see you in about an hour."

ASA Publishing Company

ASA Publishing Company

Chapter 4

Ticking Time Bomb

Parking the old unmarked Dodge in the underground police parking lot, Captain James Hawkins, a homicide detective with the Detroit Police Department, exit the car and makes his way into the dimly lit dank interior of police headquarters. Getting off the parking lot elevator on the first floor, he makes his way through the circus like atmosphere of the main lobby which never seems to fail to provide anybody that has time to look and listen, with a free freak show.

This morning's attraction features a man weighing about one hundred and twenty pounds, refusing to leave the protection of the police department because waiting for him at the door is three women . . . none of them weighing less than two hundred eighty pounds each.

"Look sir," says the officer in a very stern voice. "Your bail has been paid, so we don't any right to hold you. You have to leave."

"Man you got to be crazy," hollers the man. "You see them big bitches standing over there. They just waiting to get their hands on me, man I can't fight them big oinkers. I demand police protection."

"Sir, I haven't heard them make a threat against you, so there's nothing that I can do. Why do you think they want to do harm to you?"

"Harm my ass . . . them big bitches want to kill me . . . just because I took their F.I.A. checks and loss it at the casino. Hell, anybody can have a bad night at the tables."

"Why did you take their checks and go to the casino? Are you involved with all of them?"

"Yeah, all of them are my bitches cause I'm a playah . . . and that's what playahs do," grins the bragging man sporting a gold tooth.

"Well, I'll tell you what you do Mr. Player, your playmates are waiting for you so take your ass on out there and play" Growls the officer, getting a little angry. Grabbing the man by his coat, he walks him on tippy toes toward the door where the women are waiting. As they get close to the women, the man whirls around and punches the officer dead in the mouth.

"Now will you keep me here? I would rather take my chances with you than with them, I betcha you won't put me out now, right?"

The man was right . . . the officer pulled out his nightstick and began to play a tune on his head.

Moving on down the hall, Captain Hawkins enters his office and takes a seat at his cluttered desk. Leaning back in his old time worn desk-chair, he takes his old briar pipe from his jacket pocket and packs it with tobacco. Watching the puffs of smoke rise towards the ceiling, he tries to make sense of what had happened over the last few days. It was bad enough with the gang wars going on and the city taking a blood bath, not to mention the shock of finding out that the officer-clergyman that had been assigned to his task force to help solve the mystery of the: Heart Attack Murders . . . (the deaths of six young boys, all in good health, and all of them apparently dying of heart attacks.) had turned out to be the homocidical killer that they were trying catch. Now on top of all of that, he finds out that his lead detective on the case, Detective Samuel Simmons, was not only a homosexual, (something that he had suspected all along) but that he was involved in drug trafficking with the street gangs. And if that wasn't enough, it was the leader of one of the gangs that had saved his life in a shootout with the police-clergyman.

"If that's not enough to make me want to blow my brains out, tell me what is! The news media are having a field day with this shit. The mayor is pitching a bitch; and the commander is having a shit-fit all over my ass."

Throwing his eye's upwards, he screams, "What's next lord?!"

As if on que, there is a knock on his door. Startled out of his thoughts, Captain Hawkins pulls the old briar pipe from his mouth and growls.

"What do you want?"

Opening the door, the man peeps his head in just enough to see inside.

"Captain Hawkins?"

"Yes I'm Hawkins, what do you want? Come on in."

Entering the room and shutting the door behind him, the man stands before the captain's littered desk. He is of medium height, standing about five feet, eight inches tall, weighting around one hundred seventy pounds with black wavy hair. He has a handsomely chiseled face and a permanent tan that speaks of his Mexican descent. Flipping open a leather wallet that displays a federal badge, the man states.

"Excuse me captain, my name is Captain Manuel Lopez. I'm with the D.E.A. team that has been sent here to test and audit your confiscated drugs, and because we're conducting these tests on site, we would like to request that you be present."

Looking the man up and down, the captain nods in agreement.

"Alright, I appreciate the courtesy, I've been expecting you, just a minute."

Reaching for the intercom on his desk, he presses the button for the evidence room.

Answering the intercom comes a gruff voice.

"Evidence room, Officer Smith speaking."

"Smith, This is Captain Hawkins . . . let me speak to Officer Sharon Gates."

"I'm sorry Captain. Officer Gates didn't come in today, I'm filling in for her. Is there anything that I can do for you?"

"She didn't come in today huh, that's odd, I've never known Sharon not to report for duty. Did she call in sick?"

"I don't know sir, the Duty Officer just told me to report to the evidence room for today. I just go where I'm told."

"All right Smith, I was just asking. I'm sure she's o.k. Listen, a D.E.A. team is here to conduct some test on the confiscated drugs that we have down there. We only need the drugs that were involved in cases that have already been to trial. So get them ready, we're on our way down."

Snuffing out the lit tobacco in his old briar pipe and putting it in his jacket pocket, Captain Hawkins instructs Federal Marshal, Manuel Lopez to follow him. Going back through the lobby where three other members of the D.E.A. team join them . . . After introductions are passed around, they enter the elevator and go to the basement where the evidence room is located.

"Officer Smith," asks Captain Hawkins. "Have you got everything ready for these gentlemen?"

"Yes sir. I have everything set up over there on that table."

"Good, thank you . . . Okay gentlemen they're all yours."

Captain Hawkins and Captain Lopez take a seat at a desk and engage in small talk while the other members of the D.E.A. team began to go about their task of testing the drugs.

After a few minutes, one of the team members calls out to Captain Lopez.

"Captain Lopez, come over here for a second."

"What is it," asks Lopez."

"Like I said Captain, I think you better come over here and see this," came the man's excited voice.

Curious as to what the man is so excited about, Captain Hawkins follows Lopez over to where the team is testing the drugs.

"What's up?" asks Captain Lopez.

"Look at this Captain," says the man holding up a glass tube. "Do you see what I see?"

"What the hell!" shouts Captain Lopez. "Test the rest of them."

After the chemist perform test on the rest of the packages of drugs he shrugs his shoulders.

"They're all the same sir."

Whirling around to face Captain Hawkins, Captain Lopez hisses through clenched teeth.

"What the fuck is going on here Hawkins?"

Dumfounded by his question, Captain Hawkins stammers.

What do you mean? What do you mean what's going on? What are you talking about?"

Reaching his pinky finger into one of the packages, Captain Lopez holds it out to Captain Hawkins.

"Here . . . taste this, go on taste it."

Still confused, Captain Hawkins allows the powder to touch his tongue.

"What the hell!" bellows Hawkins spitting it out.

"Flour, this is god dam Flour. What the hell happened to the drugs?"

"That's a damn good question Hawkins, and for your sake I hope you have a damn good answer," spits Lopez.

"I don't understand it, all of these drugs were used as evidence in drug cases so I know that they were tested prior to trial, so how in the hell did they turn into flour?"

"OOHH, that's a good one Hawkins. I've been doing this shit for over twenty years and I've got my first time to see drugs turn into flour. I don't think David Copperfield is good enough to perform that trick."

"So what are you trying to say Lopez? Come on out with it."

"I don't have to say shit Hawkins, this flour is speaking loud enough for me and it's saying that somebody in this department is dirty."

Before he realizes what he is doing, Captain Hawkins grabs Lopez by the lapels of his jacket and screams.

"You rotten son of a bitch, I'll kick your ass. How dare you come into my department and accuse one of my people of being dirty."

Jumping to action, the other members of the D.E.A team separate the two men before blows can be thrown.

"Alright Hawkins, have it your way," hollers Lopez straighten his clothes. "But this isn't something you can just sweep under the rug and wishing isn't going to make it go away. I'm turning in my report and I guarantee you some asses are going to fry over this."

Captain Hawkins can only stare as the team gathers up their equipment and leave the evidence room.

"And to think, this morning I thought things couldn't get any worse. Man, this puts the whole department in deep shit, and I do mean deep. How in the hell could the drugs just disappear?"

All the while that he had been thinking, there was something in the back of his mind that was trying to come to the forefront. It just kept nagging and nagging away at him, but what was it? What was bothering him? Then all of a sudden as if it was being played over a loud speaker it came to him.

"Sharon. . . where was Sharon?"

Chapter 5

The Explosion

By the time Captain Hawkins get back to his office, his phone is ringing off the hook, he knows who it is before he answers it.

"Hello, Captain Hawkins here."

"Hawkins, what the hell is going on down there?" comes the angry voice on the other end. "I just got a call from D.E.A about confiscated drugs in our possession . . . something about flour . . . what's this all about?"

"I don't know the full story yet Chief. I was with the team when they conducted their testing and something's not right. It seems that all the drugs have been replaced with flour."

"Flour! You mean to tell me that the drugs are missing? Drugs that were in our possession, Hawkins you've got to be bull shitting me! Get your ass up here to my office and I do mean right now."

"Yes sir, I'm on my way," replies Hawkins.

Taking the elevator and exiting on the twenty second floor. Hawkins mind is racing full tilt.

"How in the hell am I going to explain to the Chief about this, right now he knows about as much about what's going on as I do."

Standing outside a door that has a nameplate on it that reads: 'Robert Macklin-Chief of Police'. Captain Hawkins hesitates and then knocks on it.

"Come on in," answer's a soft feminine voice."

Stepping inside the spacious neatly decorated secretarial office, Hawkins addresses the pretty woman that is seated behind the desk.

"Captain Hawkins to see the Chief."

"Good morning Captain Hawkins," smiles the pretty woman. "The chief is expecting you, go right on in," she said indicating a beautifully polished oak wood door.

Opening the door, Hawkins is confronted by a man seated at a massive mahogany desk. The man is solidly built, about one hundred and eighty pounds and stands about six feet tall. He is impeccably dressed in a blue pin stripped three-button suit. He has naturally wavy salt and pepper hair, which he keeps cut short. But the most noticeable thing about him was his black piercing eyes. Eyes that appear to be able to bore right through your soul.

"Come on in James, have a seat," growls the Chief.

"Now, tell me what the hell is going on in my department."

Taking a seat on the rich leather upholstered chair next to the desk, Captain Hawkins reaches for the old briar pipe but thinks better about it. Instead clears his throat and speaks in a subdued voice.

"Well actually chief. Right now all I know is what I told you on the phone. I was there when they tested the packages and all of it was flour."

"Do you know what this mean man? Have you any idea what is going to happen when this hits the papers? Those drugs fall under federal jurisdiction and that mean F.B.I as well as D.E.A. and God knows who else. This city is already sitting on top of a powder keg and these missing drugs is all it'll take to blow this whole department sky high. It's bad enough on the streets now with all these gang killings and unexplained murders, not to mention one of my own officers being mixed up in that shit. Now this?! What the fuck is happening to this department? I want answers and I want them quick!"

Riding out the storm of the Chief's verbal assault, Captain Hawkins can only nod in agreement.

"Yes, you're right Chief. I understand that we have a volatile situation here and believe me sir. I'm going to do everything humanly possible to find out exactly who's responsible for this."

"Oh no Hawkins, humanly possible isn't good enough. Do you know whom I've got to explain this shit to? The Mayor that's who. Not to mention the press and god forbid, the citizens of this city itself. So you see, my nuts are in a wringer and I don't like my nuts being squeezed like that. Because when my nuts are being squeezed, believe me, somebody else's nuts are going to feel some of the pain . . . get my drift? I want this shit cleaned up and I mean fast."

After the room is silent for a few minutes, Captain Hawkins can only nod his head up and down.

"Yes sir, I understand. I'm leaving to get on it right now."

The chief doesn't bother to look up from his desk or to acknowledge Captain Hawkins as he leaves his office. Nodding his head at the pretty secretary, his mind is undergoing a splitting headache as enters the elevator and heads back down to the jungle secretly thinking to himself.

"This is the last time lord that I'm going to ask . . . what's next?"

Chapter 6

Wolves amongst sheep

Arriving back in his office, Captain Hawkins is thankful for the peace and quiet of the dank enclosure. Removing the old briar pipe from his jacket pocket, he relights it and allows himself the pleasure of a moment of relaxation. But it is short lived as the problem at hand torments him.

"Where do I start?" then as if a light bulb had been turned on, it hit him.

"Sharon! Where the hell was Sharon?" Picking up the phone, he dials the number for the Duty Officer.

"Sergeant Sparks" bellows the voice answering the phone.

"Sergeant, this is Captain Hawkins. Did Officer Sharon Morgan call in sick today?"

"Just a minute Captain, let me check the log." After a minute he comes back to the phone and answers. "No sir. She didn't call in at all. She just didn't show."

"Okay, thanks sergeant." Hanging the phone back up Captain Hawkins mind is racing, 'Strange, something is mighty strange.' Then something dawns on him. He remembers yesterday . . . the clerk had given him a memo about the D.E.A doing a test today on the drugs and he had sent it down to Sharon in the evidence room. Now he truly had a sick feeling in the pit of his stomach.

"Man, I hope I'm wrong."

Grabbing his coat and hat, he passes through the squad room instructing one of the uniformed officers to come with him. Pulling out of the underground parking with his wheels squealing, he heads for the home of Officer Sharon Morgan.

Pulling in front of the address that he had got from personnel, he and the uniformed officer goes to the door and knocks several times. Not getting an answer, they go completely around the house peeping in all the windows. As they come back to the front, they see the next-door neighbor.

"Excuse me mam, I'm Captain Hawkins of the police department," says the captain flipping his badge, "Can I ask you a couple of questions?"

Eyeing the badge cautiously, the elderly lady approaches the two men.

"What you want me fo'? I ain't did nothing."

"No Ma'am, it's not about you. I would just like to know if you've seen Officer Morgan today."

Relieved that they wasn't there to bother her, the old woman allowed herself to relax.

"No sah. I ain't se'ed her at all today."

"Can you remember when was the last time that you saw her?"

"Yes sah, the last time I se'ed her was yesdiddy. She was going to work lak she always dus. I know cuz she had her polize suit on."

"And you don't remember hearing her coming home last night?"

"No sah, if she'ed come home las night I'd knowed it cuz my dawg always bark when she come in. No sah, she didn't come home."

Digesting what the old woman has told him, the gnawing feeling in the pit of his stomach intensifies.

"Thank you mam, we appreciate your cooperation."

Reaching into his coat pocket, he extracts a card and hands it to the lady. "If you should see or hear anything, I would appreciate it if you would call me immediately."

After the ride back to police headquarters, Captain Hawkins goes straight to his office and summons a team of detectives to join him. He pulls out the familiar old briar pipe and jams it into his mouth and starts to bring them up to date about what is going on.

"Taylor, I want you and Hunter to get a judge to sign a search warrant for her house . . . soon as you get it, I want you to take an evidence team over there and search every god dam inch of that place, and anything that looks even slightly suspicious, I want to know about."

Directing his attention toward the other two detectives, he gives out further orders.

"Jackson, you and Blevins get busy and get an A.P.B on the wire. Get her picture and description from her personnel jacket. Get the information posted right away because right now we don't know for sure if she's involved or not, but if she is, she has a good days head start on us and she could be anywhere, get moving."

After the detectives have left his office, Hawkins sits at his desk puffing on his pipe trying to put together some of the day's events. Something was clicking at the back of his mind but he just couldn't tune in on it. With all of these things happening at the same time, that little voice in his head was telling him that all of this was connected in some way, but what was the common thread?

The insistent ringing of his phone once again snaps him out of his thoughts, in a dry voice he answers, "Captain Hawkins."

"Captain, this is Detective Jackson, we just got the search warrant, do you want to meet us at Officer Gates' home or what?"

"Come to think of it . . . I sure do," says Hawkins, with excitement entering his voice. "I'm leaving right now, I'll meet you and the lab guys there."

Upon reaching Sharon's home, Hawkins arrives about the same time as the rest of the crew.

"Break out that pane of glass and you should be able to reach your hand inside and open it," indicates Hawkins to one of the uniformed officers.

After gaining entry to the house, Hawkins instructs the team, "I want every inch of this place taken apart, don't overlook nothing."

"Exactly what are we looking for Captain?" asks one of the detectives.

"Anything that might give us a clue as to Officers Morgan's whereabouts. Receipts, bank statements, letters, a diary, credit card statements. Anything that might tell us something that we don't already know."

Three hours later, Captain Hawkins is shaking his head.

"Something is mighty peculiar, all of her belongings seem to be in order. All of her clothes, even her uniforms seem to be in place. Nothing appears to be missing. There are no signs of violence anywhere in the house. It looks as if she just disappeared from the face of the earth. Uuuhhhhhmm, something's just not right," ponders Hawkins as he puffs on the old briar pipe. "One thing I do know. What ever happened, it didn't happen here. If she was taken by force, where was she taken from, and why?"

Before leaving he gives departing instructions.

"Everything that you find, get it to the lab to be analyzed. I want those bank records checked. I want this whole neighborhood canvassed to find out if any one might have seen anything suspicious regarding Sharon or this house. If she has met with foul play I want to know why, if she is on the run. . . I think I have a pretty good idea why. In other words . . . FIND HER."

That burning feeling in the pit of his stomach that he started out with this morning was now a full sized bonfire. Years of police training had taught not to ever take anything for granted, but his gut feeling had seldom led him wrong. This time he hoped to god that it was, because this time it was telling him that what he was dealing with was a wolf in sheep's clothing, or even worst, a wolf in police clothing.

The next morning as soon as he arrived at police headquarters, he had a feeling that all hell was going to break loose today, and his feeling didn't lie to him. Walking through the circus like atmosphere of the main lobby to get to his office didn't provide him with any entertainment this morning. His mood was somber and solemn and he was not in a mood to be fucked with. As soon as he sat down at his desk, his phone rang.

"Yeah, this is Captain Hawkins."

"Hawkins. This is Chief Macklin, where the fuck have you been? I've been trying to reach you all morning?" Not in a mood to be passive, the Captain shot right back.

"What in hell do you mean all morning man, it's only 6:15 a.m., I'm not even due in until eight o'clock."

"I don't give a good god damn what time you're due in, you don't have any off time as far as I'm concerned . . . the way you've let your people fuck up my department you're lucky I don't give you forever off . . . Listen, the Mayor wants us in his office for a meeting at one o'clock, it's concerning the missing drugs, but of course I shouldn't have to tell you that.

There's going to be people from the F.B.I. and the D.E.A there so I guess you know the Mayor is none too happy about this. Make sure that you're there on time and make god damn sure you bring everything that you have on this case. And Hawkins . . . you damn sure better bring something because right now you have me looking like a fool, and I damn sure don't like looking like a fool."

Hanging up the phone Hawkins opens his desk drawer and takes out a bottle of aspirin, pouring a couple in his hand, he picks up a open bottle of water that had been sitting on the desk for a couple of days and downs a couple of them. Getting on the intercom, he summons the detectives that he had working the case. The two teams enter his office and closes the door. Trying to mask his anger, Hawkins directs his questions at Detectives Taylor and Hunter.

"Okay, what do you guys have for me?"

Detective Taylor places a folder on the desk and opens it.

"Sir, these are her bank records . . . nothing out of the ordinary, she has a few hundred dollars in her savings account and it's still in there. These are records of her checking account and there's nothing unusual there either. We have records of all of her charge cards and again, nothing unusual. Oh, there was one thing . . . she has a safe deposit box. The bank teller said she visited it two days ago. We got a court order for the bank to open it, but it was empty, there was nothing in it at all."

Lighting up the familiar old briar pipe, Hawkins takes a puff, letting the aromatic scent fill the room.

"Uuuhhhhhmm. And you," said Hawkins indicating the other two detectives. "And what did you turn up?"

Detective Jackson lays his folder on the desk and reads from it.

"Okay sir, we put out the A.P.B and turned up some strange things. One of the parking lots out at the airport reported Officer Morgan's car being parked there. Detective Blevins and I went and checked it out. We had it towed to the station so the lab boys can go through it.

We also checked at the airport to see if she had bought a ticket. There wasn't one bought under her name but we believe that she's using another name because we interviewed a couple of employees in the airport snack shop and they recognized the picture that we showed them, plus a couple of the Redcaps remembered seeing her coming into the departure terminal. Yes sir, it definitely looks as if our girl has flown the coop."

Puffing on the pipe, Hawkins is forced to realize his worst fears are true, he was dealing with a rogue cop.

"With all of the people that you talked to . . . did any of them say whether she was with anybody or was she alone?"

"No sir," replied Jackson. To the best of everybody's memory that we talked to, she was alone."

"Alright guys, fine job, you're doing great but stay on it. Get back out to the airport and go thru their flight manifest again, you might have missed something. Check the tape of their surveillance cameras. Question every employee that might have come into contact with her; somebody might have over heard her say something about where she was going. And another thing boys . . . this is personal with me, there's nothing I hate worse than a dirty cop so I want this one bad, now let's go and get her."

*****

Parking on the official business lot at the Detroit City-County Building, Captain Hawkins enters the building. Passing through the guarded metal detector station, he makes his way to the elevator, enters and presses the button for eightieth floor. Following the sign that says Mayor Office, he spots Chief Macklin coming out of the men's room.

"Hey Captain, hold on for a minute. I want to speak to you for a second before we go in. First of all I want to apologize for talking to you like that this morning . . . but man, the Mayor jumped in my ass before I even got out of bed and I guess I just took it out on you, I'm sorry."

"Yeah well, I've been in the department for over twenty years and I've had my ass chewed out by better than you." The Captain said with a smile.

"Good, now we can let that shit drop. So now tell me . . . what have we got? Do we have anything that we can fire proof our asses with before we go in there?"

"My guys have come up with as much as they can at this time and they're working on some other pretty good leads."

"Well something's better than nothing. Come on, let go in and get our punishment," states the reluctant Chief.

Stepping into the Mayor's office, they are greeted by the mayor's secretary.

"Good afternoon gentlemen, everybody is already in the Mayor's office waiting for you, go right on in." Stepping through the decorative double doors with the sign that says, 'Private'. Mayor Williams, they enter and are amazed to see so many people there, at least seven or eight. After they have taken their seats, the Mayor starts.

"Good afternoon gentlemen and ladies . . . indicating the two women that are in attendance. I've called this meeting today to address some very grievous matters. Some matters that has the potential to rock the very foundation of this city as well as this administration. In case there's any of you that don't know what I'm speaking of, I'll let Captain Manuel Lopez of the Federal Drug enforcement Agency fill you in. Captain Lopez . . . if you please."

Leaving his seat and coming to stand beside the Mayors desk, Captain Lopez clears his throat.

"Aahummn, aahummn, Thank you Mister Mayor. Ladies and gentlemen. As the Mayor has just said, we're here on a very serious matter. Two days ago, myself along with a chemist team of the D.E.A. conducted a test on the confiscated drugs that were being held in the care of the Detroit Police Department. The results of those tests are as follows and I'm going to read from the report: After chemical testing was done on the samplings of drugs that were offered by the Detroit Police Department personnel, those samplings were found to be common household flour: Now I submit that this report is true and accurate because I myself was present during the testing as well as your Captain Hawkins . . . isn't that right Captain?" smiles Lopez with a instigating look in his eye.

After staring at Lopez for what seems like an eternity, Captain Hawkins replies in a strained voice.

"Yes Captain Lopez, we were present when the tests were conducted." With a triumphant glee in his voice, Lopez continues, "Thank you for your confirmation Captain Hawkins. So you see ladies and gentlemen, the testing was done quite proper and the results are irrefutable. Now taking into consideration the fact that all of those drugs were tested before the various trials that they were attached to, and found to be authentic. That leaves only one conclusion, someone in this department is a thief."

Slamming the report down on the desk to emphasize his point, he continues as he raises his voice to a loud pitch. "Someone in the Detroit Police Department stole those drugs and substituted them for flour."

The room is suddenly abuzz with the murmuring of voices and the scrapping of chairs.

"People, people, please let me have your attention." Shouts the mayor waving his arms over his head, "Just be patient for a minute, I assure you that I'm just as anxious as all of you are to get to the bottom of this. Now the only way that we're going to accomplish that is to remain calm and work together . . . Chief Macklin." Shouts the Mayor, pointing his finger at the chief, "Please come up here and tell us what you know about this situation."

Standing up from where he is seated, the Chief replies in a somewhat embarrassed stammer.

"Aahh, well sir, to tell the truth, I haven't as of yet been fully briefed on the situation," Clearing his throat, he continues on. "Aahh . . . but I've had Captain Hawkins and his detectives hard at work on it and I believe that he has some answers for us . . . Captain Hawkins, why don't you let these people know what you've found out?"

Walking to the front of the room in what seemed like the longest walk of his life, Hawkins thinks to himself.

"You spineless son-of-a-bitch. So you're going to shift all of the weight on me huh? Aah well, what else is new?"

Standing in front of the room with a folder in his hands, he began, "First of all I want to explain to you that we've only had knowledge of this situation for two days, but here's what we've got. As captain Lopez so eloquently explained." He made sure he put emphasis on *eloquently*. "The drugs that were tested produced a positive for flour. Now the lead that we're following is this. Officer Sharon Morgan was in complete control of the evidence room where the drugs were kept. She was the only one that had control of what came in or what went out of that room, so it is our theory that she was instrumental in the drugs being switched.

Now here's the interesting part . . . she's missing. We conducted a search of her home yesterday but that didn't turn up anything unusual, but we did put out an A.P.B. and we got lucky. We were able to locate her car. It was parked in one of the long-term parking lots out at the airport. We also conducted an investigation at the airport. We interviewed some employees who recognized her photo as someone that they saw in the departure terminal. That's all that we have right now but I'm sure that you understand that this an ongoing investigation and there's still a lot of things to check out, we're waiting for the lab guy's to give us the report on her car; we're still going through the passenger manifest at the airport; we're going through her bank records. There's still a lot of work to be done, but rest assured, we are working on it and we're not going to let up until we have all the answers."

At the end of his report, Hawkins lowers his head and goes back to regain his seat. That was the hardest thing that he had ever had to do in his life, give a report on a dirty cop and it made it ten times as hard because this dirty cop was one of his.

"That was a very heartwarming speech Captain," sneers Captain Lopez.

"But I think that you're missing the point. What we want to know is how did this happen in the first place? All I've heard you mention was one cop. This Officer Sharon Morgan. Who was working with her? It's been my experience that when you find one dirty cop, you dig deep enough and you'll find another."

"Whoa there Lopez," shouts Mayor Macklin, "I think that you're going a little too far insinuating that there's crooked cops in this department."

"Too far?!" shouts back Lopez, Ooohhh Mr. Mayor, I haven't gone nearly as far as I'm going to go. By Captain Hawkins own admission, you have one bad seed in the bunch and like I said, if you dig deep enough you'll find more. Let me be honest with you Mr. Mayor, those drugs were federal property and I'm a federal officer. So it's my duty to not only find out what happened to them, but how and why. And believe you me; I'm going to do everything in my power to make sure that I get the job done. Now Captain Hawkins and the rest of your boy's in blue may only have the integrity of this department in mind, but I don't. I'm not bound by the protective rules of your little in house boo boos, so frankly I don't give a damn whose head comes under the chopping block, I'm going to do my job."

Glaring at Captain Lopez, The mayor had to take several moments to compose himself. As he looked around the room at all the open mouths and astonished looks, he knew that this wasn't the time or place to vent his anger at this motherfucker who had the unmitigated gall to come into his sanctuary and in front of his subordinates dress him down. Instead he put on his best political smile.

"Captain Lopez, I'm sure there's been some misunderstanding. I guarantee you that there is no one in this department that would dream of impeding your investigation of this or any other case. As a matter of fact I'm issuing an executive order right here and now that the full resources of the Detroit Police Department is at your deposal."

Taken by surprise at the way the Mayor melted under his attack, Lopez stammers.

"Why, uuhh thank you Mayor, that's very kind of you and I do appreciate your cooperation. Maybe I did get a little carried away but I just want you to understand the seriousness of this matter, and I do take my job serious, and with keeping that in mind, on the Federal Government's behalf, I'm going to spear head this one myself. I want all of your people that are working on this case to coordinate all of their findings with me. I want to know everything that is discovered and I want it cleared with me before it is acted on. I want to know everything about Officer Sharon Morgan from the time the doctor first told her mother it's a girl . . . up till the last time she took a shit."

Grimacing through clenched teeth, the mayor responded, "Not a problem Captain Lopez. Chief Macklin will be glad to help you set up command in his office and assist you in any way that he can . . . right chief?"

Reluctantly, the chief answered in the affirmative, "Sure Mr. Mayor, whatever you say."

"Thank you Chief, and now ladies and gentlemen, that's about all we have for right now. And for you members of the press, I'll be holding a public press conference at noon tomorrow. Chief Macklin if you would hold on for a minute, I would like to have a word with you."

Chief Macklin sits uneasy until everybody has left the room. With only him and the Mayor there, the room seems as if it has grown to be the size of the Grand Canyon. With a timid voice, he breaks the ice.

"Well sir, what do you think?"

Peering up from his desk, the Mayor has blood in his eyes, in a bellowing voice he asks, "Are you kidding me Macklin? You've got the balls to sit there and ask me what do I think! Did you hear the way that grease ball motherfucker disrespected me? Right here in my own house! And now I have to play nursemaid to that bastard! And you know who I hold responsible for this shit . . . you, that's right, you."

"But Mr. Mayor, how is this my fault?"

"I'll tell you how . . . you are the head of the police department and it's your job to know what's going in your own house. If you were doing your job all of this bullshit wouldn't be happening in this city . . . all of these gang killings, that god damn freak detective of yours that got himself killed, and now this . . . drugs being stolen by your own cops right from under your own nose . . . and you ask me what do I think? I think I should fire your sorry ass, that's what I think."

Feeling like a little kid that had just got caught with his hand in the cookie jar, Chief Macklin speaks in a subdued voice, "I admit that there's been a little more than the usual problems in the department, but it's nothing that I can't handle sir. All I need is a little time."

"Time . . . you have less time than I do Macklin. I'm the one that has to answer to the press and to the citizens of this city and when they hear about this latest fuck-up, they're going to want my ass on a silver platter. But I'll tell you what . . . before they get my ass, I'm going to have yours, I hope you understand where I'm coming from . . . so go on and get that motherfucker set up in your office and get to the bottom of this shit so that I can be rid of his ass."

Chapter 7

You owe me one

Pouring over the piles of reports on his desk, Captain Hawkins puffs on his old briar pipe as he tries to read between the lines on each one.

"This is the damndest case I've had since the: Heart-attack Murders. Somehow I have the strangest feeling that they are all related in some way . . . but how?"

His thoughts are interrupted as Chief Macklin barges into his office.

"What have you got Hawkins? It's been three days now and you haven't brought me shit. The Mayor is about to have a shit fit and you're not giving me anything to get him up off my ass . . . and don't even start me talking about that god damn Captain Lopez, man, he has taken over my office. I can't crack a fart without him wanting to smell it. So tell me, what the fuck are you doing to clear this shit up?"

Hawkins thinks to himself, 'Why you sniveling weak-ass bastard, all you can think about is yourself.' Instead he replies, "As you can see Chief, I've been working on this case night and day. We got the lab reports back on Officer Morgan's car and the only thing that turned up was her uniform, other than that there was nothing unusual found in it. But finding the uniform does confirm one thing . . . she's on the run, otherwise why would she leave that behind? My theory is that she had some clothes with her, and when she found out that there was going to be an audit of the drugs she knew that her time was up, so she left work, changed clothes in her car and went to her bank . . . took whatever that was in her safe-deposit box . . . went to the airport and she was gone."

"Gone, Gone where? See Hawkins, that's the stupid kind of shit that I'm talking about. You tell me that she's gone . . . hell man, I know that the bitch is gone!" shouts an irritated Chief Macklin, "But where? What the fuck are you doing about finding out where she is? Don't you understand what I mean when I say that the mayor is in my ass over this? I can't go to him with some weak ass theory about what I think she did. I need for you to find her and bring her thieving ass back here and I do mean in a hurry. And look Hawkins, I know that Lopez want to know everything that's going on in this department, but fuck that. This is still my house and I call the shots."

"So as soon as you find out something, I want to know about it before he does . . . understand where I'm coming from?" says the chief with a wink.

"You see captain. The mayor is not going to be mayor forever and I've got political aspirations of my own, and this could just be the vehicle that can ride me into that office. So look at the big picture . . . if I become mayor that leaves my job open, and as mayor whom do you think I would automatically appoint as the new chief? So you see, it's in both of our best interest to keep the solving of this case in house, you know the old saying . . . you scratch my back and I'll scratch yours."

'Yeah chief, I know exactly where you're coming from. I scratch your back and you'll stab me in mine,' thought Captain Hawkins. Instead he replied, "Yes sir chief, whatever you say, I'll let you know as soon as I have something."

"Wonderful Hawkins, I knew I could count on you. And I know that I can count on you to keep our little talk under your hat."

Before going out of the door he turns around, and with a shit-eating grin he states, "And Captain, don't take too fucking long to clean this shit up."

After Chief Macklin has left his office, Hawkins rears back on his chair and puts his feet upon it. Puffing on his pipe, he wonders where to go next with his investigation.

"I'm getting nowhere fast with this one and it's not helping me at all to have that chicken-shit chief riding my ass." Then as if someone had turned on a light bulb inside of his head, he snapped his finger. "Wait a minute, I'm going about this thing all wrong."

Grabbing his desk Rolodex and looking up an address, he grabs his hat and heads for the elevator.

Pulling the unmarked Dodge out onto the street, he heads for west Warren Avenue. Passing by the dilapidated buildings, the same ones that he had passed by for years without any kind of particular feelings; this morning he was hoping that amongst them he would find some help. Matching the address on the piece of paper in his hand with the old beat up building in front of him, he parks his car and stares at the sign over the door . . . "G.M.O. Club (gang member's only)."

Entering the one story building, his nose is assaulted by the smell of fresh paint. It takes a moment for his eyes to get adjusted to the bright lights illuminating from the new fixtures hanging from the ceiling, and baring the entrance to the interior of the building is a door that prevents him from going any farther. Ringing the doorbell, he is greeted by a young black kid of about fifteen years of age. Before opening the door the kid asks, "What you want?"

"I'm here to see Roy White," answers Hawkins.

"Roy White!" repeats the kid, "Ain't no Roy White here."

Taking out his badge, Hawkins flashes it to the kid and states, "Tell you what son, just open the door and I'll see for myself."

After looking at the badge for a moment, the kid reluctantly opens the door.

"Alright dawg come on in, but I'm telling you . . . ain't no Roy White here."

Walking through the door and into a large gymnasium sized room; Captain Hawkins is amazed at the beehive of activities that are going on. There's a couple of pool tables that are occupied by young boys shooting a game. There is a boxing ring with two boys engaged in a sparring match. There are various kinds of exercise equipment being used by a bunch of kids. Spotting a group of kids gathered around a desk, Captain Hawkins approaches them and asks, "Do any of you know a guy by the name of Roy White?"

Hearing the sound of the name being called, the kid sitting at the desk looks up at the Captain and with a surprised look in his eye and stands up.

"What you want him fo'?"

"I just want to talk to him for a minute . . . you might say he's a friend of mine."

Walking away from the table and gesturing for the captain to follow him, the kid enters an office and closes the door. Taking a seat on a sofa and motioning for the chief to do the same, he grins.

"And what can I do fo' you captain?"

"First of all, let me congratulate you on the fine job that you've done with this place Jasper."

Grinning with pride, Jasper adds, "Thanks captain but you need to congratulate yo' self. Did you see all those kids out there? Those kids be from all different gangs in the city, but they can come here and kick it together. I didn't think it could work but look at it. There's living proof it do. And they owe it all to you cause this be yo' idea. But captain, 'bout that

Roy White thang; everybody know me as Jasper, so let's keep it like that, huh?"

"Ha, ha, ha," laughs the captain good-naturedly. "I was just having a little fun Jasper, your secret's safe with me. And like I said, I'm proud of what you've done in such a short period of time, I knew I was right about you. But listen Jasper, I'm here today for another reason. I need help."

"What you mean you need help?" asks Jasper, as his voice gets serious, staring the captain in the face, he waits for an answer.

"Jasper, ever since that night that you saved my life, we both knew that there was going to come a time when we would have to talk. Well that time has come."

With a suspicious tone to his voice, Jasper asks, "Talk about what?

"Jasper, I'm going to say some things that I know you're not going to like, but I have to say them anyway. And it's especially hard now in light of what you're doing for these kids."

"Captain, whatever you got to say, say it cause I don't like the way this be going."

"All right Jasper, since that night I've done a lot of investigating into your background and I know for a fact that you were supplying The Diablo's with cocaine and I know that you were getting that cocaine from Detective Simmons. And now I think I know where he was getting his from."

Jumping up from the sofa, Jasper paces back and forth across the small office.

"So this be what yo' bullshit be 'bout. You did all this good shit just so you could stick me with a dope case. Ain't you 'bout a bitch! Here I be thinking, man, finally a white person that really give a shit and all the time all you be doing is setting me up fo' a case." Sticking his hands out to be cuffed, Jasper hollers, "Go ahead mutha-fucka, take me in!"

"Wait a minute Jasper, I haven't said anything about arresting you, why don't you let me finish saying what I have to say?"

"What else is there fo' you to say? You say you got the goods on me, well go on, take my ass to jail but I ain't saying nothing till I gets a lawyer."

Once again Captain Hawkins tries to calm him down, grabbing Jasper by the shoulders, he pushes him against the wall and hollers, "God dam it Jasper, listen to me! I didn't come here to arrest you, I came here because I need your help, now hear me out." Releasing his hold on Jasper, Hawkins continues, "All I want is for you to hear me out and then you can make your own decision, what do you say?"

Puzzled by his words, Jasper squints his eyes to mere slits as he stares at him and nods in the affirmative.

"All right man, go on and say what you got to say."

Not bothering to sit back down . . . now it's Captain Hawkins that paces the floor.

"Okay Jasper, thanks. Like I said, I thoroughly investigated your background from the time that you first started the Diablo's, up through your association with Detective Simmons. I'm not going to go through everything about your past because that's not the reason that I'm here. The reason that I'm here is because my ass is on the hot seat to solve a case that involves the drugs that you were getting from Simmons."

"Now hold on captain. What makes you . . . ?" interjects Jasper.

Not giving him a chance to finish his question, Hawkins continues, "Like I said Jasper, I know that you was getting your drugs from him, but that's not the issue. What I need to know is, who was working with him? Who was he getting his drugs from?"

"Why you coming to me with some shit like that? You say you know I was coping dope from Simmons. First of all I ain't admitting to shit, but if I was, what make you think I know who his connect be?"

Taking out his old briar pipe and lighting it, Hawkins let the aromatic smoke swirl around the office as he retakes a seat on the sofa. Speaking in a low voice, he says, "I don't know Jasper, I'm taking a shot in the dark but I think that you know a lot more about that dope than I do. Let me make myself perfectly clear about this. If I wanted to bust you on something believe me, I could have done it before now."

Taking another puff on the pipe and blowing the smoke into the air, he continues, "Jasper, I owe you my life and that's why I decided to give you a chance to make up for some of the wrong that you've done. Looking around at what you've done with this place and these kids, I know that I made the right decision. So now that means that you owe me. Not only that, I think that you owe yourself a lot more."

Jasper asks with a perplexed look in his eye, "What you mean by that? Okay maybe I owe you fo' not busting me, but what you mean I owe myself a lot mo?"

"Jasper, you're a natural leader. Hell you've already proven that by what you did with the Diablo's, and that was for all the wrong reasons. Now just think what you can do with that kind of leadership if you put it to good use."

After thinking for a minute, Jasper replies, "Uuuhhmmm, so what you be saying is you want me to be a snitch."

"Jasper, the hell with that snitch shit. That's dumb ass talk for dumb ass losers. No, what I want you to do is help me to help keep these kids in here alive by keeping that shit off the streets. I want you to help me give you a chance that nobody else gave you; a chance to make a difference in this city, a chance to really become a leader and lead these kids to something positive instead of an early grave, so if you think that's what snitching is forget this conversation and let whatever happens happen. But just remember . . . you could have made a difference."

"Wow captain, you lay some heavy shit on a nigga. Why don't you let me think on this fo' awhile?"

"I would love to have the luxury of you taking your time Jasper, but I don't. Like I told you before, my ass is sitting on top of a volcano that's about to erupt. I need your help and I need it now."

Scratching his head, Jasper is in deep thought.

"Okay Captain let me ask you this. If I do help you, do I have yo' word that you aint gon' jam me up with none of this shit?"

Pointing the stem of his pipe at Jasper, the Captain answers, "I told you before, I don't want to jam you on anything, I just want your help . . . so yes, you have my word."

With a sigh of resignation, Jasper gives in.

"Alright Captain, I'm gon' trust you this time, like you say . . . I owe you one, so what you wanna know?"

"Great Jasper," says Hawkins with glee in his voice, "That's great, first of all tell me something, did Simmons ever tell you where he got his drugs from?"

Pacing the floor for a minute, Jasper takes time to think.

"Uuumm, I cracked on him a few times about who his connect was, but man, Simmons wasn't the kind of dude that you wanted to push too far, so when he told me not to question him 'bout his business, that's what I did."

"Are you sure that he never mentioned any one that he might be associated with? Anything at all, Jasper think hard, this is very important."

"Naw Captain, I can't think of anybody. In fact the only person I ever se'ed him with was that night that broad caught him sucking on my Johnson."

"What broad? What night? Where did this happen?" asked Hawkins with excitement creeping into his voice.

With a twinge of embarrassment, Jasper relates to the captain the events that had taken place that night at Detective Simmons' apartment.

"And I could hear her yelling and screaming while she was laying some serious shoe leather to his ass, but that's all I know cause I was getting the fuck up otta there."

"Listen Jasper, did you get a good look at her? Do you think you could identify her if you saw her again?"

"Yeah, if I saw her again I'd recognize her, like I said, I was looking right in her face when Simmons had my shit in his mouth."

Captain Hawkins reaches into his coat pocket and takes out a picture of Sharon and hands it to Jasper.

"Do this look like her?"

"Look like her my ass! That is her! That's the bitch that whipped Simmons ass."

Hawkins was happy as a kid on Christmas morning, he had his connection. Now he knew for certain that Sharon was instrumental in the missing drugs.

"Listen Jasper, I want you to think about this for a second. Did you ever see both of them together transacting a drug deal?"

Scratching the side of his head, Jasper goes into deep thought.

"Uuuummmm, Not exactly saw them doing business but that ain't too hard to figure out. The last time I copped some jive from Simmons, he was a key short so he told me to come over to his crib later that night and pick it up, now when I get there, my shit is straight, so I figure she must be the one that brought it to him. Who's she anyway?"

"Her name is Officer Sharon Morgan. She was in charge of all of the drugs in the evidence room down at headquarters, it's my belief that she and Detective Simmons were partners in their own drug business and that's where the drugs were coming from."

"Well I'll be damn, so that's where Simmons was getting that good shit from."

"Jasper, everything that we've discussed is to be held in the strictest confidence, I gave you my word that your name won't be included in anything that is going on and by the same token I insist that anything that we talk about stay between us. Do I have your word?"

"Hell yeah, that ain't no problem. As long as you ain't trying to jam my ass up, yeah, you got my word."

"Thanks Jasper, I appreciate that. Look I've got to go now, but I'll be back around to see how things are going."

Chapter 8

Inside Fighting

Arriving back at his office, Captain Hawkins chews on the stem of his old briar pipe and digest what he has learned from Jasper. Picking up his phone, he dials Chief Macklin's office and the syrupy sweet voice of his secretary greets him.

"Chief Macklin's office, how my I help you?"

"This is Captain Hawkins, I would like to speak to the chief."

Transferring the call to the Chiefs desk, the Chief answers in whispered tones.

"This is Macklin, what can I do for you?"

"Chief, this is Captain Hawkins. I've got some information that I think we should run by Captain Lopez."

Speaking in a low whisper, Chief Macklin cautions Hawkins not to speak too loud.

"What kind of information?"

"I found out some things about the missing drugs that he might want to know."

"Damn Hawkins, didn't I tell you that we can solve this thing without putting Lopez into the mix? I told you what plans I have and I'll be god dam if Lopez or anyone else is going to get the credit for cleaning up my department, so fuck Lopez. Whatever information you have, give it to me and we can work this thing together. I'm on my way to your office."

Over hearing his name being mentioned, Captain Lopez looks up from the desk that he occupies in the Chief's office.

"What's up Chief? Did I hear you call my name?"

Surprised that his whispered conversation had been heard, Chief Macklin stammers to cover up his mistake.

"Huh, call your name, oh no, no I was just reminding one of my detectives that as soon as he comes up with something, to make sure that he runs it by you first, that's all. Uh listen Lopez, I have to go and check on a few things and I should be back shortly, if you need me before I get back, hit me on the radio."

Taking the elevator down to Captain Hawkins office, the Chief is in a foul mood as he barges into the office and slams the door behind him.

"Okay Hawkins, what have you got?" asks the Chief with a snarl in his voice.

Taken aback at the sudden invasion, Captain Hawkins pulls his feet off the desktop and takes the old briar pipe from his mouth and stammers for words. After repeating what he had found out from Jasper (*without mentioning Jasper's name*) he finishes his report and wait for the Chief's reaction.

"So that's how they were doing it! That's good police work Captain, That's good shit," says a jubilant Macklin clasping his hands together. "But that is only the beginning of what we have to do. We have to find out where that bitch is and what she did with the drugs and the money. Now I want you to listen and listen well to what I'm saying Hawkins. Forget all that shit about reporting anything to that pain in the ass Lopez, this is our house and we'll do any housekeeping that needs to be done. So whatever you get, you give it to me. Understand?"

"Yeah Chief, I get the picture, whatever I get, you'll be the first to know."

"Now you're talking like a man with a future," smiles the Chief.

After Chief Macklin had hung up the phone and made an excuse to leave his office, Captain Lopez was sure that he had heard Macklin speaking to someone about something that they had found out about the missing drugs. He was also sure that Macklin was bullshitting him along and had no intensions of sharing information about the case with him. But being the veteran cop that he was, he knew that the best way to find out what was going on was to play dumb and wait. He observed the gleeful look on Chief Macklin's face when he returned to his office, a look that had not been there when he left.

"Hey Chief you look mighty pleased with yourself, you got good news or something?"

"What? Oh it nothing, just a little joke one of the guy's was telling me."

Staring at the Chief with eyes that seemed as if they were boring holes straight through to his sole, Lopez asks.

"So you didn't find out anything about the case huh?"

Walking over to Lopez's desk, the Chief puts his face inches away from his and hisses.

"What the fuck are you insinuating? If you have something to say, say it."

With a cold stare, Lopez looks right back at him and replies in a calculated voice.

"I'm not insinuating anything Chief, and I've already asked you what I wanted to know, but if you didn't hear me I'll ask you again, did you find out anything about the case?"

Words of anger begin to creep up his throat like bitter gall. But because he was under rule of the Mayor, he had to swallow the anger along with his pride. He knew now was not the time to vent, he had too much to lose to let this mutha-fucka get the best of him. He knew the best thing that he could do at this time was to just be cool.

"No Captain Lopez, I didn't find out anything."

Settling back into the plush desk chair, Captain Lopez tap's a pencil against the desk as he continues to stare at Macklin.

"Thanks Chief, that's all I was asking."

Chapter 9

Inside Out

The annoying ringing of the doorbell awakens Captain Hawkins from the catnap that he was taken in front of the television. Glancing at his wristwatch, it tells him that it is 9:15 pm.

Going to the door and peeping through the peephole; he is surprised to see whom it is. Opening the door and closing it behind them, he greets his visitors.

"Good evening gentlemen . . . Jasper, what the hell are you and L'll Hammer doing here?"

"We 'pologize fo' coming to yo' crib like this Captain but something been bothering me since you came to the club today."

"Something like what Jasper? I thought that we had an understanding."

"Oh no, it ain't nothing like that Captain, we still cool 'bout that. It's just some things that I can't get straight in my mind."

"You boys come on in and have a seat," says the Captain motioning them toward the sofa. "What kind of things is it that you can't get straight in your mind?"

"Well I don't know zackly how to start so I'll start with what used to be my dawg, Rico. I already told you the story 'bout how me and Rico ran the Diablo's . . . man we were tight. I knowed Rico had my back when I couldn't count on nobody else, so you got to know how surprised I was when he flipped on me."

Wondering where all of this was leading to, Hawkins asks, "What made Rico turn on you?"

"That's what I'm getting to. It wasn't money cause he was getting plenty of that. So the only thing that could turn him was a bitch."

"Now come on Jasper it couldn't be that. With the kind of money that you guys was making I'm sure getting sex wasn't a problem."

"See, you don't understand where I'm coming from. I'm not talking 'bout pussy, I'm talking 'bout a bitch. Rico's head got swelled up by a bitch and that bitch's name is Tonya."

Trying to think of a delicate way of putting it, Hawkins wanted to ask Jasper what the fuck did this have to do with him.

"Jasper, that's over and done with. Maybe you're better off just letting it go."

"Just hear me out Captain. Let me finish and then tell me what you think. Like I said, this Ho' name Tonya be Rico's bitch. I should've known from the jump that she was trouble. After all the drama between the Diablo's and The Satan Disciples cooled down, me and L'll Hammer did some investigating and guess what we found out? We found out that Tonya and Rico planned all of the killing that went on between the two gangs so they could take charge, but Rico didn't know that Tonya was playing his ass too cause she had hooked up with Baldy and was planning on killing him. But anyway I'm getting ahead of myself so let me back track a little. After Sharon kicked Simmons ass, The Diablo's needed a new dope connect. So Tonya, being the smart bitch that she is, she cut into Sharon so she could take Simmons place. Now Tonya is one freaky ass bitch, so it don't take too much guessing to know how she convinced a rejected love starved bitch like Sharon to see things her way."

By this time Captain Hawkins is sitting on the edge of the sofa with his mouth wide open, with excitement filling his voice he speaks, "Wow, are you serious? This Tonya, you say she was buying drugs from Sharon! Are you sure? Where is she now?"

"I wish I knew Captain. I had real love fo' Rico and that bitch turned him into a rabid dog. If I find her, that bitch is mine. But as far as I see, she don' split with an ass load of cheese and dope."

"Do you think she and Sharon might be together?"

"Well like I said Captain, that Tonya be one freaky ass bitch and if Sharon got half way hooked on that pussy as my dawg Rico was, I'd say it was a sho' bet."

Sitting in silence for a few minutes, Hawkins digests the incredible information that has just been revealed to him.

"Well I'll be damned, this throws a whole new slant on this case. Jasper I want to thank you guys for this info. And listen, I need you to do something more for me. I need you to put together a list of everybody that she knows . . . friend's . . . relatives . . . enemies. If you know of anybody that she even winked at, I want his or her name on that list. If you've ever heard her talk about relatives or friends out of town I want to know who and where."

"Whoa there Captain, slow yo' roll, we said we'd help you but we ain't cops."

"Hell Jasper I know you're not cops, you're just what I need. You and L'll Hammer can go into places and talk to people that a cop never could, man don't back out on me now."

Finally L'll Hammer speaks, "Captain I been listening to yawl's jabbering 'bout this and that but I got's this to say. I ain't no snitch but them dudes that got killed in them dope houses was my hommies. So if Tonya be responsible fo' that shit, count me in cause she gots to pay."

"Good. I'm glad to hear you say that L'll Hammer but I also want you to keep in mind that we're not on a vigilante hunt, this is a police matter and it will be conducted as one. All I want you to do is find out all you can about where she might be and report back to me . . . understood?"

With a bit of resignation in his voice, L'll Hammer nods his head in the affirmative.

"Yeah Captain. I dig where you be coming from and I know I owe you fo' what you don' fo' me with Miss Bauer. But like I said, those boys was my hommies and that bitch be responsible fo' them being dead . . . so I ain't promising shit. That mutha-fucka is got to pay."

"Don't worry Captain," interjected Jasper. "Me and L'll Hammer gon' play it straight with you. We don' fucked up enough shit in this city, now it's time to do something right, we gon' play it yo' way. Whatever we find out we'll let you know."

Chapter 10

No back up

Sitting at his desk puffing on the familiar old briar pipe, Captain Hawkins is in a state of confusion over what he has learned from Jasper. For over twenty years as a cop, he has always played by the book and that means following orders. Now he is in danger of his ass being put through the wringer because of the chief not wanting him to follow the orders of the Mayor to share all information with the D.E.A. Captain Lopez.

"It's a situation of damn if you do and damn if you don't. Well to hell with it," picking up his phone he dials the chief's number.

"Chief Macklin's office," comes the syrupy voice of the secretary.

"This is Captain Hawkins, may I speak to the Chief please?"

"Yeah Hawkins, what do you want?" asks the irritated voice of Macklin as he answers the phone.

"Chief, I've got some more information on the missing drug case, but to tell you the truth, I'm a little uneasy about not sharing this info with Captain Lopez, after all that order came straight from the mayor himself."

"Goddam it Hawkins, how many times do I have to tell you to just do as I tell you to do?" barks Chief Macklin trying hard to keep his voice to a whisper, "I'm on my way to your office."

Observing the chief's reaction to the phone call, Captain Manuel Lopez stares at him as Macklin gets up from his desk.

"Got something going chief?"

"Huh, naw, I'm just going to check on something, I'll be back in a few."

"Say chief, speaking of running out for a few minutes, I need to get to a dentist, can you recommend one?"

Thumbing through his Rolodex, Macklin hands Lopez a card that says, 'Dr. Bernard Sanders, DDS'.

"This is my dentist, he's the best there is. Give him a call and tell him that I sent you and I'm sure he'll see you right away."

Macklin breathe a sigh of relief because he was sure that he was getting ready to go through some more shit with Lopez. He was more than glad to give him the name of his dentist. Dr. Sander's office was way out in Southfield on Evergreen and twelve Mile Road, so that should keep him out of his hair for the rest of the day.

Leaving Captain Hawkins office after being filled in on the latest information that he had, Macklin is in a foul mood from giving Hawkins a berating. Before he can reach his office, his cell phone rings.

"Yeah, who's this?"

"Never mind who this is," came the voice on the phone, "But I have some information I think you can use."

"Listen whoever you are. I don't know how you got my number and frankly I don't give a fuck. In case you didn't know it, I'm Chief Macklin of the Detroit Police and I don't have time to play games, so either state your business or go fuck yourself."

"Don't get so high and mighty chief. I know exactly who you are. Now I'm going to mention one word, and if that word doesn't interest you, all you have to do is hang up. The word is . . . Sharon."

The name Sharon exploded like a live bomb inside of Macklin's head.

"Okay, you have my attention, what do you want?"

"Now that's a little more civil. See, it doesn't cost anything to be polite do it? If I could deliver Sharon to you would you consider owing me a favor at a later time?"

"Owing you a favor? What kind of favor? Man I don't even know who I'm talking to."

"Who I am doesn't matter at this particular time. What does matter, and I'm sure you will agree, is that you get that mess cleaned up in your department about the drugs. Now chief I know what your political aspirations are . . . you want to become Mayor. And I'm sure that if you single handily busted this case that would go a long way toward accomplishing that goal."

"How do you know so much about what's going on in the department? The only way that you can be so informed is that you are a member of the department in some way. What do you want from me?"

"Like I said, as mayor of this fine city you could be in a position to return the favor. Do we deal or what?"

"You said you can deliver Sharon to me?"

"Let me put it to you this way, I can tell you exactly where she is."

"Okay my man, if you can tell me where that bitch is, you've got a deal, but let me warn you, if you're trying to pull something slick I'm going to be your worst nightmare. Whoever you are I'll find you."

"Damn Chief, just when I thought we could be friends there you go with the threats again. I tell you what, why don't I just give this information to Captain Lopez and that way he can get the credit for solving the case and you won't have to be mad at me . . . alright?"

"Wait a minute, just wait a minute," blurts Macklin afraid of losing the key to the case. "Look, I'm not threatening you. But I don't even know who I'm talking to so I'm a little cautious, I'm sure you can understand that."

"Alright chief, apology accepted I'm glad we're friends again. Now here's the deal. Sharon is going to be at the house that Rico and Tonya lived at over on Westwood street."

"You mean that house that those two gang members were found dead in?"

"Yes, that's the one. Now Tonya is hot so she's not going anywhere near the place, but she stashed some money somewhere in the house that only she knows where it is. But I've got a flash for you; Sharon is going to pick it up for her at eight o'clock tonight. And to make sure they don't arouse any suspicion, she is coming alone. Now if you think about it chief, that's the good part. If she's by herself that means that you can take her by yourself without any help and just think how that will make you look, man you'll be the talk of the town."

Chief Macklin's thoughts are pure delight as he gets a mental image of tomorrow's headlines . . . Chief of Police single handily solves Detroit's drugs scandal.

"Yeah I like that, in fact I love it. Now are you sure she's going to be there at eight? And by herself?"

"That's the word that I have and it's from reliable sources. What I would recommend is that you get there about an hour early and surprise her when she gets there. But you know chief, just to be on the safe side, why don't you take a few uniforms with you, that way there shouldn't be any slip ups."

"Look my friend, I've been doing this shit for a lot of years so I don't need anybody to tell me how to do my job. You gave me all of the information that I need so let me handle it my way. And another thing. How do I get in touch with you when this is over?"

"Don't worry about that chief, like they say in the movies . . . don't call me, I'll call you."

Hanging his phone up, the chief is elated as he goes into his office, he can't believe his stroke of good luck, somebody is actually laying the case right in his lap.

"Who could it be? I bet it's somebody in the mayor's office, that's it, it's got to be somebody in the mayor's office who knows that I'm moving up and they want to get in on the ground floor. Well whoever it is, he's one smart son-of-a bitch, and I can use people like that."

"What's up chief?" greets Captain Lopez as Macklin enters his office. You look mighty pleased with yourself. Anything I should know about?"

"Naw Lopez, just doing a little daydreaming that's all," replies the Chief gleefully. "I thought you would be at the dentist by now, did you call him?"

"Yes, as a matter of fact I did and he can take me today, thanks for the turn on." Looking at his watch, Lopez jumps up from his desk. "Oh damn, I've got to go, my appointment is in less than half an hour and I've got to go to Southfield, I'll see you tomorrow."

"Not a problem," cracks Macklin. "Tell Dr. Sanders I said hey."

Chapter 11

Bad Decision

Checking his watch, it tells him that it's 7:00 p.m. taking a flashlight from the glove compartment and sliding it into his pocket. Chief Macklin makes one final check of his service revolver before getting out of his unmarked car. Having parked around the corner from the house so as not to tip his hand, he pulls his trench coat tight around him to brace himself against the brisk fall night air as he walks at a fast pace toward the house.

Reaching the house, he cautiously makes his way to the rear where he uses a locksmith's tool to jimmy open the door. After gaining entry, he quickly closes the door behind him and pulls out the flashlight making sure that he keeps the light aimed at the floor in order not to attract attention from the outside.

The house had been thoroughly ransacked. All that the police had not destroyed in their investigation of the murders that had taken place there; vandals had completed the job. They had stolen all of the furniture, the kitchen cabinets, the kitchen sink, the bathroom sink, the carpet off of the floor. They had stripped the house of all the copper plumbing and even the toilet.

"Damn, a swarm of locus couldn't have picked this place any cleaner," thought the chief, "If they have some money hidden anywhere in here it has to be one hell of a hiding place."

Checking out the hallway closet, he decides that would be the ideal place to wait for Sharon to arrive, if he left the door slightly ajar, he could see her if she came from the front or the back. Taking a seat on the closet floor, he checks his watch again before turning off the flashlight.

"7:25 . . . about thirty-five minutes to go, well, might as well make myself comfortable."

The time passes quickly as the chief daydreams about the glory days that are before him, resulting from him and him alone solving the missing drugs case.

He is startled from his daydream by the faint sound of keys turning the lock on the back door. Silently he stands up in the closet, his breath coming in short gasps. He can hear his own heartbeat. Sweat began to form on his forehead as the sounds of cautious footsteps come down the hallway, "Click, click, click."

Peering through the slight opening of the closet door, he can barely make out the figure of someone passing by the closet. With his heart beating like a jungle drum and sweat pouring down his face, the chief slowly pulls out his gun and pushes the closet door open. Steeping into the hallway behind the figure, he screams in a voice so loud that he didn't recognize it himself.

"Freeze motherfucker. If you so much as twitch I'll blow your black ass too hell. Put your hands up where I can see them and turn around."

Slowly the figure turns around to face the chief. But because of the lack of light in the house, the chief can't see the face clearly, but assuming that it's Sharon, the chief allows himself to relax a little. Squinting his eyes to try to make out the face, he brags, "So miss smart bitch, I guess you're not so smart after all. You might have out smarted all of them other sorry ass excuses for cops, but you fucked with the wrong nigga this time. I'm the top cop in this fucking city so that means your ass was working for me . . . so guess what? When you decided to fuck with the city, you were fucking with me and I don't take kindly to anyone fucking with me."

To emphasize his meaning, Chief Macklin delivers a quick backhand slap that sends the figure staggering against the wall. Sticking his gun into his holster, he pulls out his flashlight and approaches the figure.

"Hold your fucking head up so I can get a good look at you bitch."

Training the light on the figures face, he notices that the wig that she is wearing has been knocked crooked. Reaching out his hand he grabs the wig and in one swift move, pulls it off. With the flashlight trained on the face, the chief's jaw dropped in disbelief.

"What the fuck? You're not Sharon! What the fuck is going on here? What are you doing here?"

"You're right chief, I'm not Sharon, Damn, you got that right on the first guess. I guess you're smarter than I thought. But listen, before you go and do something stupid like going for your gun, why don't you take a look at what I have in my hand."

Turning the flashlight toward the figures hands, Chief Macklin starts to sweat profusely as he see the large semi-automatic hand gun that is pointed at him.

"Okay old bean, this is how we're going to do this. You're going to give me the flashlight and then you're going to give me your gun. Now I know what you're probably thinking," says the voice in a mocking tone, "But trust me, there's no way in hell that you can come out with your gun before I can pull the trigger on mine. So let's do this sensible, alright?"

As per orders, Chief Macklin hands over the flashlight and then very slowly hands over his gun.

"Alright you've got everything. Now tell me what is the meaning of this bullshit? Why are you doing this?"

"Well to tell you the truth chief, even as stupid as you are, you're still getting to close to something that you shouldn't be, and that could be a problem, a problem that I don't need."

With a sinking feeling in his guts, the chief tries to make sense out of it.

"Too close to what? Man I don't know anything about what you're talking about. Why would I make problems for you?"

"It's a little too complicated to go into right now, I just don't have the time. I'd better just get this over with."

The chief's eyes go wide with fear as the sweat pours down his face; he can barely utter a sound.

"Wait a minute, you mean you're talking about killing me? Man that's crazy! I haven't done anything to you. Plus there's something that I bet you didn't think of. I've got back up just waiting for my call. If I don't make that call they'll be here quick."

"Now come on chief, who do you think you're fooling? You're to god dam greedy to share a collar with anyone. No my man, you don't have any backup."

Just as Chief Macklin starts to protest, he notices a quick flash of bluish-white flame that erupts from the mouth of the silencer that is attached to the muzzle of the semi-automatic that is pointed at him. It strikes him as peculiar that all of a sudden there is no more fear; it seemed strange that everything is so peaceful; without sound or pain. As the bullet tears through the front of his forehead, traveling through the brain and making it's exit through the back of his skull tearing a chunk of it away. Yes . . . death is peculiarly peaceful.

Going over to the body, the figure makes sure that his work is done. He wipes clean his fingerprints from the flashlight and leaves it there. He repeats this procedure with the chief's gun and anything else that he might have touched.

Satisfied that everything is in order, he exit's the house and disappears into the night.

ASA Publishing Company

Chapter 12

Trouble on the home front

Puffing on his old briar pipe, Captain Hawkins brief moment of peace and quiet is abruptly interrupted by the ringing of his desk phone. Putting down the stack of reports that he had been looking through, he answers it in an irritated voice.

"This is Captain Hawkins, what can I do for you?"

"Good morning Captain Hawkins, this is Captain Lopez. I'm sure you remember me. I'm the guy that is working out of Chief Macklin's office, you know, from the D.E.A. . . . the guy that your Mayor ordered you guys to work with on the missing drugs case," says Lopez in a sarcastic voice.

Biting his lip in order to keep his cool, Captain Hawkins answers in a controlled manner, "Yeah Lopez, I remember who you are, what do you want?"

"Well that's good, I'm glad to hear that I haven't been completely forgotten, for a minute there I wasn't so sure."

"Alright Lopez, enough with the smart shit, what do you want?"

"What I want is a little cooperation, and so far I'm not getting jack-shit from anybody. We're supposed to be working this case together and so far no one has reported anything to me. Now I don't claim to be the sharpest knife in the drawer, but I do have sense enough to know that somebody in this department has found out something and that means I'm being left out."

"Wait just a damn minute Lopez, I've got a good memory. I remember when we were down in the evidence room when the drugs were discovered missing . . . you did everything but accuse me of being dirty. I didn't appreciate it then and I don't appreciate it now. Let me make something perfectly clear to you, there is a thing called the *Chain of Command*. Now in case you don't know what that is I'll explain it to you. My detectives report whatever they find to me. I report to my chief and he reports to whomever it is that he reports to. So if you have a problem with being left out of the loop, I strongly suggest that you take it up with him."

"You bet your sweet ass I have a problem with it, and I would love to take it up with your chief except I can't seem to find him. It's past noon and he hasn't shown up for work yet. I've called his house and I don't get an answer, I believe he's on to something and I want to know what it is."

"Is that what this shit is all about? Because you can't find the chief?!"

Before he could catch himself, Captain Hawkins throws his head back and laughs out loud, "Ha, Ha, Ha, Ha. So your little feelings got hurt because the chief didn't tell you when he had to go take a piss. Well, if you can't keep up with him, I don't know what to tell you."

With a voice dripping with malice, Lopez replies, "Thank you for your cooperation Captain, have a nice day."

Hanging the phone up, Captain Hawkins resumes looking through the reports on his desk, all the while that little nagging voice in the back of his head is bothering him, 'That fucking Lopez gets on my last nerve. I know he's right about the chief not sharing any information with him, but what the fuck am I supposed to do? I follow the chain of command, I report to the chief. After that it's not my business. Fuck it . . . let them work their own little pissing contest out. But I've got a funny feeling that I just can't put my finger on. The chief haven't reported for work and its afternoon, that's not like him, he's too ambitious not to be on time, uuuhhhmm, not like him at all.'

The next morning as Captain Hawkins pulls his unmarked Dodge into the underground Police parking lot, he notices that the space reserved for Chief Macklin's car is empty. Checking his watch, he makes a mental note of the time; 6:45.

"Uuhhmm, the Chief is usually here by now."

Getting on the elevator, Hawkins starts to press the number for his floor but instead presses the floor of Chief Macklin's office. Approaching the desk of the syrupy voiced secretary, Hawkins asks if the chief is in.

"No I'm sorry Captain. He hasn't arrived yet, and frankly, I'm a little worried. He didn't check in at all yesterday and that's not like him."

"You mean you didn't hear from him at all! Did you call his house or his cell phone?"

"Yes sir, I tried both numbers and didn't get an answer. I even left voice messages for him to return my calls, but nothing."

"The last time you saw him; did he mention anything about meeting anyone?"

"No sir, the last time that I saw him was day before yesterday, he left here about six o'clock and he didn't say anything about meeting with anyone."

"Did you check his itinerary for yesterday and see if he kept any of his appointments?"

"Yes sir, as a matter of fact some of his appointments called here to see if he was running late. So the answer is no. He didn't keep any of them."

Taking the old briar pipe from his coat pocket and placing it in his mouth, Hawkins clamps down on the stem as he concentrates on what he has just learned.

"Uuuhhhmmm, tell you what I want you to do Mrs. Rodgers. Check with all of his appointments for today and let me know if any of them has spoken to him. In the meantime, I'm going to check on a few things. Oh by the way, where's Captain Lopez?"

"He's at his desk in the Chief's office, go on in."

Entering the Chief's office, Hawkins approaches the desk where Captain Lopez is sitting going over some papers. It irritated Hawkins to know that Lopez refused to acknowledge his presence by not looking up from what he was doing.

"Excuse me Captain Lopez," says Hawkins with a heavy dose of sarcasm in his voice. "I'm sorry for interrupting your busy day, but I need to ask you a couple of questions."

Reluctantly, Lopez looks up from his desk.

"Yeah Hawkins, what do you want?"

"It seems like no one has seen the chief in a couple of days. I need to know if you have spoken with him."

With a look of mock exasperation on his face, Lopez exclaims, "Moiré, now how in the world would little ole' me know when the chief is going to take a piss? Remember, these are the same questions that I asked you yesterday and you practically told me to go fuck myself . . . well I'm extending you the same invitation. Get the fuck out of my office."

Standing there fighting back the urge to tear into Lopez and beat the shit out of him, Captain Hawkins controls himself and speaks softly.

"I can't quite put my finger on what it is Lopez . . . but there's something foul about you. I don't know what it is, but it will come to me . . . trust me, one day it will come to me."

Closing Chief Macklin's office door behind him, Hawkins goes back to syrupy voice's desk.

"One more thing Mrs. Rodgers, you say the chief left his office around 6:00 p.m., what time did Captain Lopez leave?"

Checking her daily log, she finds the entry.

"He had a dentist appointment with a Dr. Bernard Sanders out in Southfield at 5:00 p.m., so he left around 4:15."

"Thanks Mrs. Rodgers. I'll be talking with you a little later, if you hear from the chief let me know."

Taking the elevator down to his floor, Hawkins enters his office and makes a few calls. The first one is to the motor pool to find out what unmarked unit the chief had checked out. Upon getting that information, he called the dispatcher to post an All-Points Bulletin on the vehicle. Next he orders a detective team to check out the chief's residence.

"If he's not there canvass the neighborhood, talk to his neighbors, find out if any of them have seen him. As of right now we don't know if anything is wrong, but we have to treat it like it is, so that means you use every precaution."

A S A   P u b l i s h i n g   C o m p a n y

Chapter 13

Too Close To Home

All day long, Police Headquarters had been a beehive of activity, even more so than its usual chaotic drama. The mood was in a very serious state, as news of the missing Police Chief spread like wild fire. The report from the detectives that had checked out Chief Macklin's apartment had come back negative, everything from the outside was normal, no sign of forced entry, no broken glass, nothing. And to gain entry to the inside, they would have to get a court order . . . which was in progress.

The news had already been leaked to the press, and their reaction was the same as when any piece of news had the possibility of being sensationalized, they went into a feeding frenzy.

Police Headquarters was being bombarded with teams of reporters from the various television stations, all of them wanting to know the answer to the same question. Where was the Chief of Police?

An impromptu press conference had been set up in one of the briefing rooms to try and keep the press under control as best as could be. Captain Hawkins had been placed in charge of the meeting with instructions to tell the truth about what they knew but to keep it simple. Standing at the podium in front of the room full of reporters, Captain Hawkins began his speech:

"First of all ladies and gentlemen, I want to thank all of you for coming out here today. But let me make one thing perfectly clear; I'm sure that you've heard all kinds of rumors about the absents of Chief Macklin, but as of right now that's all we can tell you . . . he's absent! We don't have reason to believe that it's anything other than what I'm telling you. Now if there's any questions?"

A tall blond haired fellow that the Captain remembered from being interviewed by him during the *Heart Attack Murders Case* spoke in a loud demanding voice.

"Yes Captain, I have several questions. First of all, how long has the Chief been missing?"

"Well sir. Like I said the Chief is absent. There is a difference between missing and absent . . . the Chief has been absent for two days."

"Come on Captain, that's just a play on words and you know it. But anyway, has there been any signs of foul play?"

Deciding to let the snide remark pass, Hawkins addresses the other question.

"Sir, if there was any signs of foul play, then he wouldn't be classified as absent . . . then he would be missing. Does anyone else have any questions?"

"Yes sir, Thelma Johnson from Channel 5 News. Is this a common practice for The Chief of Police to be absent for two days without anyone knowing his whereabouts?"

"No Mrs. Johnson, it's not common practice for any police officer to be absent without notice, but until we do a full investigation into the matter, we don't have reason to believe anything negative."

"I thank you for that Captain," replies the reporter, "But we're not talking about just any officer, we're talking about the Chief of the whole Detroit Police Department. And it strikes me as a little odd that he could be missing for two days without anybody seeing or hearing from him and all you can say is, he's absent?"

Feeling perspiration beading on his forehead, Hawkins is temporary at a loss for words; he hated these damn press conferences.

"Miss, I can appreciate your concern, and believe me, I understand how easily it is to jump to conclusions. But as I said, this matter is under investigation and that's all we know at this point. Now if our investigation turns up anything new, we will certainly let you guys know. Once again I thank all of you for coming out today, but that's all we have for now."

After the press has left, Captain Hawkins has barely got back to his office when his phone rings.

"Captain Hawkins speaking."

"Captain this is Detective Taylor. We just got word from that A.P.B. that went out on the Chief's car. It's been spotted over on the Westside, my partner and me are heading over there now. Just thought you might want to know."

"Good work Taylor, damn right I want to know. After you get over there and check things out, let me know what's going on, I'll call the lab guys and have them meet you there. Make sure they go through that car with a fine toothcomb."

Propping his feet upon his desk and rearing back into his chair, Hawkins pulls out the familiar old briar pipe and sticks it into his mouth. Deciding not to light it, instead he bites down on the stem as he sifts through the activities of the last few days in his mind, and wonders out loud.

"Uuhhmm, I wonder where that asshole of a Chief is? With all of the shit that's been going on lately, it really not like him to not have his nose dead in the middle of everything . . . unless he's gotten onto something about the missing drugs like Lopez suggested and don't want to share the information. But what could it be that would cause him to be missing for two days? Naw, none of it makes any sense. Maybe I should let Lopez in on what's happening, but on second thought, he's only here to work on the missing drugs case. This doesn't have anything to do with him so fuck him, the less that I have to do with that son-of-a-bitch the better I like it."

Several hours later, the Captain's phone rings again.

"Captain Hawkins speaking."

"Captain this is Detective Taylor again. We're here where we found the chief's car. The lab guys have done everything that they can do with the car over here. We're having it towed to the lab so they can do more extensive examinations. According to them from this search, they didn't find anything out of the ordinary. We interviewed some of the residents on the street and to the best of their memory the car has been parked here about two days.

We checked with the departments Human Resource Division to see if the Chief had any relatives that lived on this street . . . nothing, nothing in his personnel file about this neighborhood. We talked to everybody that we could in the area, nobody saw him park here, nor did they see anybody around the car."

"Did the car look as if it had been stolen and parked there? Maybe someone car jacked the Chief somewhere else and drove the car and left it there," says Hawkins digging for answers.

"At this point anything is possible sir. Maybe after the car has been thoroughly gone through in the lab, we'll have more answers."

"Yeah you're right Detective Taylor. But until we have a handle on exactly what's happening, I want every vacant house in the area thoroughly searched. Missing drugs are one thing, but a missing police chief is a whole different matter, I want this mystery cleared up and I do mean fast. The press has already gotten wind of it and I don't want them blowing it all out of proportion. Make sure you make out your report and have it on my desk as soon as possible . . . and thanks, good job."

Chapter 14

Black day for the city

The voice coming from the TV in his office had the effect of someone pouring ice water down his back. The mayor's eyes are glued to the set.

"We interrupt our regularly scheduled program to bring you this breaking story. We are on the scene at a house on Westwood Street on Detroit's west side. A neighborhood that we have from reliable sources, has been searched trying to find the where about of Detroit Police Chief, Robert Macklin. The chief has been missing for two days; two days in which no one has seen or spoken with him. There are about a dozen police cars on the scene, so something is definitely going on inside of the house. Right now the police won't let us get any closer, but we will stay on the scene and keep you up dated as this story develops. Now, back to your regularly scheduled program."

Mayor Williams is dumbfounded, at a loss for words, he picks up his phone and dials Police Headquarters. Reaching Chief Macklin's office, he is greeted by the syrupy voiced secretary, "Chief Macklin's office."

"This is Mayor Williams, let me speak to the Chief," blurts the mayor in an angry voice.

Hearing the rage in his voice, the secretary is more than a little intimidated.

"I'm sorry Mr. Mayor" she stammers. "But Chief Macklin isn't in, can I take a message?"

"Too hell with a message, you can tell me where the chief is. And what's all this shit on the TV about the chief being missing?"

On the verge of tears from the rage in the mayor's voice, she stammers, "I don't know where the chief is Mr. Mayor. No one has seen him in two days. And as for what's on TV, I don't know sir, I don't have it on."

"Well if the chief isn't there, who in the fuck is in charge? It's a god damn shame that when I want to know what's going on in my own fucking police department, I have to hear about it on the TV."

With the tears now running freely down her cheeks, the secretary sobs out another apology.

"I'm sorry sir, I told you everything that I know. Captain Hawkins was up here asking about the chief and I told him the same thing, so maybe you might want to talk to him."

"All right . . . all right, stop crying, I'm just trying to find out what's going on, if you hear from the chief, tell him to call me right away." Hanging up from the secretary, the mayor dials Hawkins office.

"Captain Hawkins speaking."

"Hawkins, this is Mayor Williams, what the fuck is going on? I just talked to Macklin's secretary and she told me that he's been missing for two days, and what's all this shit on TV about something going on at some house on the west side? Why in the fuck am I the last mother fucker in this god damn city to know what's going on in my police department?"

"Mr. Mayor, I just found out today that the chief has been missing for two days, so up until now I didn't know there was anything to report to you about. As a matter of fact I just got a call from one of my detectives that is at the house and I'm just leaving to go there myself."

"You damn well better be on your way there, and listen, when you get there take charge. Keep those fucking reporters away from that house until we know what's happening, and as soon as you do, call me and let me know what's going on."

Making his way through the line of squad cars, Hawkins parks his unmarked Dodge as close to the house on Westwood as he could. Getting out, he shoves his way through the crowd of people that has gathered there.

Addressing one of the uniformed officers, he starts to bark out orders, "Get some help and put up barricades around this house, get these people back behind them and I do mean now! Who's the senior officer here?"

"That would be Sergeant Green sir, he's over there on the steps."

Walking over to a uniformed officer with sergeant stripes on his arm, Captain Hawkins began to question him with anger in his voice, "Sergeant, do I have to tell you police procedures? Why isn't this place barricaded off? You've got so many people crowded around here, I can't tell the civilians from the cops. But I'll deal with you later on that . . . right now, what do we have here?"

A little ticked off at being reprimanded in front of his men, Sergeant Green replies in a dry tone, "I don't know yet, we had personnel doing a sweep of all the vacant houses in this area and a team of uniforms found a body in this house. We have a forensic team inside checking it out."

"All right Sergeant, I'll take command from here. You stay out here and make sure that everything that needs to be done is done properly."

Entering the house that is now filled with forensic and evidence techs, Hawkins makes his way down the hallway towards the front, which is brightly lit from the light bars that has been sat up. He stops and stares at the figure lying on the floor being photographed by the evidence techs. One look at the highly polished shoes and expertly tailored suit that it is wearing; nobody has to tell him that the body is that of Chief Macklin. Silently he thinks to himself, 'Holy shit, the press is going to have a fucking field day with this one. How in the world do you explain the killing of a Police Chief? I don't care how you look at it, this is a black day for the city.'

Speaking to the forensic tech, he inquires, "Do you know what was the cause of death? And how long would you say he has been dead?"

"I would say the cause of death was one shot through the head, and judging by the state of rigor mortis that has set in, I would say about 48 hours, give or take a few," explains the tech, "But all this is just preliminary until we can get him to the coroner's office and do an autopsy."

Stepping over to a corner of the room, Hawkins takes out his cell phone and dials the mayor. After his secretary connects the call, Hawkins visibly shaken by the discovery, stammers, "Mr. Mayor, this is Captain Hawkins, I'm at the house of the crime scene, and yes sir, the body is Chief Macklin."

The mayor's end of the phone goes silent for what seems like an eternity. Finally he speaks, "Look Captain," mumbles the mayor, "Uuummm, I tell you what, make sure that no one talks to the press about this until we get a handle on what's going on. I want you in my office first thing in the morning. Now I'm counting on you to keep the lid on this, understand?"

"But Mr. Mayor, the press is already here, there's TV crews all over the place."

"But my ass!" shouts the mayor, "What they think is going on and what they know is going on are two different things. I said keep a lid on it and goddamn it that's what I mean. If I so much as think that someone over there says something that they shouldn't have, I'll have their ass on my breakfast plate by tomorrow morning. Do I make myself clear?"

"Yes sir perfectly clear. I'll make sure that nobody talks to the media," replies the captain in a defeated tone.

A couple of hours later, the body has been removed, all evidence has been collected, police crime scene tape has been attached to the house and everybody has left except Captain Hawkins. Sitting alone in his car, he stares at the house as his head is filled with questions, 'What was the Chief doing here? Why was he here? Who was here with him? And last but not least, who killed him and why? The Chief definitely was not one of my favorite people, but he was still a cop and he didn't deserve to die in a gutted out abandon house like a gutter rat.'

After sitting and thinking for a few more minutes, Hawkins starts the car and heads for home, dreading that he has to face the mayor in the morning.

Chapter 15

House Cleaning

Parking the unmarked Dodge on the executive parking lot of the City County Building, Hawkins goes inside of the building and presses the elevator button for the mayor's floor. He had barely entered the reception area, and introduced himself to the secretary, when he hears the mayor's booming voice.

"If that's Captain Hawkins, send him in."

Out of habit, Hawkins reaches for the old briar pipe, but thinking better about it, he leaves it in his pocket, takes his hat off and steps into the mayor's office. With a humble voice he speaks, "Good morning Mr. Mayor, you wanted to . . . ?" Before he can go any farther, the mayor goes into a tirade, pushing himself up from his desk, he thrushes a newspaper in Hawkins face.

"Have you seen this?!" yelling at the top of his voice he continues, "Go ahead, read it!"

Staring at the headlines of the paper, Captain Hawkins is stunned. In big bold print it reads . . . "**Even the police are not safe in Detroit.**"

With spit forming at the corners of his mouth, the mayor continues his verbal assault on Hawkins in a loud boisterous voice, "Do you know what this kind of publicity will do to this city? I told you I wanted a lid to be placed on this . . . well thanks a lot."

"Sir, I did what you asked me to do," whines Hawkins in a half apologetic voice. "Not one police officer said anything to anyone from the news media. But you have to understand, there were fifty or sixty people from the neighborhood gathered out there and people are not stupid. They know that there was a search going on for the chief and with all of those police cars suddenly on the scene, it didn't take much to put two and two together. I did my job, it wasn't us."

Seeing the sense in what the Captain is saying, the mayor calms down a bit. "Yeah, I guess you have a point there. It's just that, too god dam much is happening too god dam fast in this police department. First we have young boys being mysteriously killed by what turns out to be a homocidical fake pastor, slash, cop. Then we find out that one of our detective's is a gay drug dealer that has been supplying the gangs with dope. Then we have open warfare between the street gangs that left a blood bath in the streets of this city. Then we have drugs in our possession that magically turns into flour, and it turns out that one of our officer's is responsible for that little trick . . . Oh by the way, what the fuck are we doing to find her black ass? Now comes the granddaddy of them all, the Chief of Police of the City of Detroit is found murdered in an abandoned house.

As mayor of this city I ask you, what does that make me look like? I'll tell you what it makes me look like . . . an incompetent ass hole that don't know how to run a city, that exactly what I look like, and I don't like looking that way. Now here's what I'm going to do . . . I'm appointing you as the new Police Chief, effective immediately. And as the new chief, I'm going to hold you personally responsible to do some house cleaning. There are too many bad apples in the barrel, I want them weeded out. But first things first . . . I want all available resources to be put on finding Chief Macklin's killer. I don't give a fuck if you have to turn this city inside out, nobody kills a cop in my city and gets away with."

At a loss for words, Hawkins mumbles, "Me, Police Chief?! Sir with all due respect, I don't know if I'm ready for that."

Going back into a tirade, the mayor slams the newspaper on his desk and points his finger at Hawkins and snarls, "God damn it man, don't go acting like a sniveling puppy, show some backbone. Chief Macklin is dead and somebody has to take his place. Now in case you didn't notice, I didn't ask you if you wanted to be chief, I said you are the new chief, any questions?"

Realizing that any objections would be fruitless, Chief Hawkins accepts his new appointment. "No sir, and thank you, I'll do the best job that I can. Oh, there is one question . . . Captain Lopez."

"What about him?"

"Well sir, since I'm the new Chief, I assume that I'll be moving into Chief Macklin's office; now you also have Captain Lopez sharing that office too . . . so do I have him working on this case with me or what?"

"Hell no!" spits the mayor, "That son-of-bitch is there for one thing and one thing only; the missing drugs case, anything else is none of his god damn business. I don't like the idea of those nosey ass feds sticking their god damn noses in my business anyway. Naw, anything concerning the drugs, share with him, anything else is our business. I'll have my secretary get the memo out right away letting everyone know that you're the new Police Chief. Now remember what I said, I don't care what it takes, I want Macklin's killer caught."

Chapter 16

New Sheriff in Town

Arriving back at Police headquarters, Hawkins is shocked at the number of TV trucks and reporters camped outside the building. Driving past them, he goes to the back and enters the underground parking. He had barely stepped from the elevator when reporters thrusting microphones into his face mob him, hollering at the top of their voice; everybody was trying to ask him questions at the same time. There was one pretty young black woman, about forty years old that stood out from the rest . . . what made her so noticeable was her size and spunk, even though she weighed less than one hundred pounds, and stood about five feet even, she had refused to be intimated by the larger reporters surrounding her. She pushed her way to the front of the crowd and got face to face with Hawkins and began firing questions.

"Captain Hawkins, what have you found out about the murder of Chief Macklin? Do you have any leads?"

Looking deep into the woman's eyes, Hawkins carefully chooses his words before he speaks in a calculated manner, "As of right now, the death of Chief Macklin is under investigation. And I'm sure that all of you know that I can't comment on any details of a case involving an open investigation."

"We can appreciate that Captain, but is there anything that you can tell us?"

"Not about the case itself, but rest assured, as soon as we have anything that we can share with you, we will."

"What about the office?!" shouts the woman, "Who will be taking the chief's place?"

With a look of acceptance on his face, Hawkins answers, "As of a few minutes ago, the mayor appointed me as the new Chief of Police. Now that's all I have for you at this time ladies and gentlemen. And if you will excuse me, I have to get to work."

Walking at a fast pace, trying to stay ahead of the reporters that are following him, Chief Hawkins reaches the elevator and closes the door behind him. Getting off at his floor, he acknowledges the various . . . congratulations on becoming chief, from the detectives and uniformed officers he passes on his way to his office.

Once inside, he puts his feet upon his desk, takes out the old briar pipe, lights it, and lets the smoke swirl around his head as he tries to take stock of all that has happened. His thoughts are interrupted by a knock on the door.

"Come on in!" shouts Hawkins.

"Excuse me Captain . . . I mean Chief," smiles the man dressed in workmen coveralls. "Congratulations on your promotion. They sent me up here to assist you in getting your things moved into the chief's office. I've got boxes and a flatbed dolly to load all of you stuff on, so I'm ready when you are."

Face to face with the actual act of moving into the chief's office, it finally dawn on Hawkins that he is the new chief.

"Yeah, thanks Willie. I guess we might as well get the show on the road. Just start packing everything into the boxes."

For the next couple of hours, Hawkins and Willie spend the time between moving Chief Macklin's stuff out and moving Chief Hawkins stuff into his new office. Chief Hawkins notices that all the time that he has been coming back and forth into the office, Captain Lopez haven't spoken a word. Finally after he had finished and he was alone with him. Lopez grins and says rather dryly, "I'm not going to go through all that congratulation bullshit. You don't care for me, and the feelings mutual, so let's get one thing straight. I've been assigned to this office to work on the missing drugs case and now since you're moving in here, I guess we'll be seeing a lot of each other. But keep this in mind. I expect the same thing from you that I expected from the late Chief Macklin, anything that you find out about the case, I want to know about it before you do anything. Other than that, you stay out of my way, and I'll stay out of yours, understood?"

Moving over to his new desk, Chief Hawkins sits on a corner of it and takes out his old briar pipe, packs it with tobacco, lights it and blows out a cloud of smoke before he speaks in a slow, calm ice cold voice, "Let me explain something to you Lopez. Ever since you came here, you've been a disrespectful, antagonizing, pain in the ass, son-of-a-bitch.

The mayor is a politician, so I can understand why he has to put up with your ass . . . he has to do things in a political manner. Chief Macklin, he had political ambitions, so I understand why he kissed your ass. Now take me, I've been a cop for over twenty years and that's all I ever want to be, I have no political ambitions whatsoever. You have been assigned to this office to work on the drug case, fine. I'll follow orders and work with you. But I'm going to tell you one time and one time only. The next time you disrespect me . . . The next time you so much as look at me sideways, I'm going to drag your bitch ass out on Gratiot Avenue and put my foot so far up your ass . . . you'll be picking shoe leather out of your teeth for a week. Understood?"

Narrowing his eyes to mere slits, Captain Lopez stares at Hawkins as if he could see through his sole. He starts to reply, but seeing the cold look on Hawkins face, he rethinks his actions, and returns to reading the folder in his hands.

Feeling good about finally being able to put Lopez in his place, Chief Hawkins steps out of his office into the reception area and speaks with his new secretary. "Mrs. Rodgers I would like for you to notify all of the department heads and let them know that I expect every one of them to be in the briefing room in an hour for a meeting, no exceptions."

"Yes Sir . . . Chief Hawkins, I'll do that right away," she replies in a voice that is eager to please. "And Chief, I'd like to express my condolences on the loss of Chief Macklin, he was a fine man. If you need any help getting settled in, just let me know."

"Thanks Mrs. Rodgers, that's all I need for now, but I'm sure you're going to be very helpful in getting me used to all this."

An hour later, Chief Hawkins is standing in front of a lectern in the Detroit Police Department's briefing room; a room that is filled with the various department heads.

Clearing his throat, he began, "Good afternoon ladies and gentlemen. I'm sure that by now all of you have heard what has been going on. For those of you that haven't, I've called this meeting to dispel any rumors and lay out the facts. Chief Macklin is dead. He has been murdered by person or persons unknown, and in light of this, the mayor has appointed me as the new Police Chief. I know that all of your departments have been working on different cases, well as of right now, all of that is on the back burner," pausing to stick the old briar pipe into his mouth, he continues, "That's right, I don't care what case you're working on, put it on the shelf.

The only thing that anyone will be working on until farther notice, will be finding Chief Macklin's killer. I'm not saying that what you're working on is not important; I am saying that someone in this city has killed a police officer and right now finding whoever it is, is the most important thing that you'll ever do. I want all of you to coordinate your investigations with your people and keep me advised of what's going on at all times. We have a lot of work to do in this department, so we don't have forever to crack this case. Plus the news media are already on our asses about this and rightfully so, if a police chief isn't safe in our city, who is? So let's go to work people and find the killer."

Chapter 17

Wild Wild West

For the next several weeks, The Detroit Police Department declared open warfare on any and all illegal activities in the city. Crime took a nosedive as a force of over two thousand police personnel combined their talents and dedication towards one goal; to find out who murdered Chief Macklin.

They didn't leave a stone unturned in their efforts to solve the case; every after-hours 'Joint' in the city was shut down. Every known 'crack house' was raided. Every prostitute on the street was picked up and questioned. Every two-bit hustler in the city was brought in and interviewed. Every known felon in the city was taken into custody on suspicion and questioned, all to no avail. After hundreds of interrogations and after following up on hundreds of tips, nothing. Not one solid lead. It was if some mysterious being from another planet came to Earth, killed Chief Macklin, got back in their spaceship and flew away. Never in the history of Detroit law enforcement had there been such a sweeping and professionally carried out investigation, yet it still yielded nothing for their efforts.

During the past few weeks, the relationship between Chief Hawkins and Captain Lopez had remained tensed at best. Neither man speaking to, nor even acknowledging the existence of the other unless absolutely necessary.

"Well Mr. Hawkins," Captain Lopez says nonchalantly, "I got my orders today and it appears that I'm being reassigned. So it looks like you won't be seeing my smiling face around here anymore."

Rage instantly erupts from Chief Hawkins at the obvious disrespect of being addressed as 'Mr.' instead of 'Chief'. With the speed of a much younger man, Hawkins crosses the distance between Lopez's desk, and his own. Before Lopez realizes what is happening, Hawkins grabs his necktie and winds it up in his hand until it is choking him. With venom attached to every word, he strains his words through clinched teeth.

"You grimy little bastard! I told you before what I would do if you ever disrespected me again. Did you think I was lying?" spit the Chief, wrapping the tie tighter around his hand until Lopez's eyes were beginning to bulge in his head. "The fact that you are getting the fuck out of my office is the only thing that is stopping me from keeping my promise of wrecking your sleazy ass, but don't push me too far . . . let this be your last warning."

Unwrapping the Tie from his hand, Chief Hawkins releases his hold and backs away from the desk. As the necktie is loosened from around his neck, Lopez takes deep gulps of air and starts to cough uncontrollably. Straining for words in between coughs, he whispers, "Man, are you (cough, cough) crazy? What the hell are (cough, cough, cough) you trying to do? Kill me?!"

With fire in his eyes, the chief replies, "It's still not too late for that to be accomplished motherfucker. The best advice that I can give you is for you to get your shit and make your move now."

Forty-five minutes later, Captain Lopez and all of his belongings were gone from Chief Hawkins' office.

"Chief Hawkins," came the syrupy voice of the secretary from the desk intercom, "I have some papers that need your signature. May I come in?"

"Yes, of course Mrs. Rodger's. Come on in," answers the chief as he pulls the old briar pipe from his mouth.

Opening the door to the chief's office, Mrs. Rodgers enters carrying stack of papers in her arms. Placing them on Hawkins desk, she thumbs through them, indicating the ones that needed his signature. After getting all of the necessary signatures, Mrs. Rodgers picks up the stack and heads for the door. Half way there, she stops and turns back around.

Hesitating before she speaks, she says in an apologetic tone, "Chief Hawkins, excuse me if I'm speaking out of place, but I couldn't help but hear what was going on in your office between you and Captain Lopez. It might be wrong for me to say this . . . but I'm glad he's gone. I didn't like him and I didn't trust him."

Looking at her with a quizzical expression on his face, Hawkins retorts, "I can understand why you might not like him, he's not a very likeable person. But what do you mean, you didn't trust him?"

Stepping from foot to foot in an uneasy manner, the secretary searches her brain for the right words. After all, she had just started working with Hawkins and she didn't know how he would react to her putting in her two cents. "Well for one thing, he was always questioning me about things when the chief wasn't around, and after questioning me, he would ask me not to tell him about anything that he asked me."

"What kind of things was he asking you about?" inquired Hawkins with interest in his voice.

"Most of it was general information. It wasn't so much about what he asked, as it was about how he asked," replied Mrs. Rodgers, wondering if she was over stepping her boundaries. But deciding that if she had gone this far, she might as well continue. "But what really puzzled me, was the way he would always wait until the chief left his office, and then he would go through his desk and file drawers. And he would always ask me whom the chief's mail was from. Now if you ask me that was being a little too nosey."

"Did you ever speak with Chief Macklin about these things?"

Lowering her eyes towards the floor, she answers in a pleading tone that begged for understanding. "No sir I didn't. But you have to understand, I hadn't been working for Chief Macklin but a little while, and I found out quick that he wasn't very easy to talk to. Plus that, Captain Lopez was a federal agent, so what was I supposed to do? I have three kids to look out for, so I need my job. I just couldn't put that in jeopardy, so I kept my mouth shut."

"I'm not judging you Mrs. Rodgers," says the chief in a sympathetic voice. "I can understand your reasons for not saying anything. But now that we're going to be working together, I want you to know that you can talk to me about anything that's happening around here, okay?"

With a sigh of relief, Mrs. Rodgers manages a smile. "Okay sir. And thank you for understanding."

"That's quite alright Mrs. Rodgers, but let me ask you something before you go. If you can remember, the last day that you saw Chief Macklin, can you recall him talking to anyone about where he was going after work?"

Going into deep thought, Mrs. Rodgers replies, "Uuummm, now that you mention it, there was something. I remember Chief Macklin standing out in the hallway, and I could hear him talking on his cell phone. I couldn't hear him real good because the door was shut . . . but I did hear him mention the name Sharon, and that she was supposed to be picking up some money. Now I don't know what that means or who he was talking to."

With the mentioning of the name Sharon, Hawkins attention was at full alert.

"Sharon! Are you sure you heard him say Sharon? Think Mrs. Rodgers. What else did you hear? Come on and have a seat," demands the chief excitably motioning her to a seat beside his desk.

Settling herself onto the chair, Mrs. Rodgers digs into the deep recesses of her memory. "Yes sir, I'm positive that I heard him say Sharon. It seems like I could make out him saying something about her picking up some money at eight o'clock at Tonya's house."

Removing the old briar pipe from his mouth, Hawkins yells with excitement, "Mrs. Rodgers I could kiss you! You have just given me the first solid lead that we have in the chief's murder. Now I want you to listen and listen good. I don't care who ask you anything about what you have just told me, don't say nothing to nobody."

Unaware at how she had helped, nevertheless, Mrs. Rodgers was happy that she had done something to please her new boss and pledged her loyalty to him. "Don't worry Chief, you have my word."

As soon as the secretary had left his office, Hawkins was dialing the mayor's office. As soon as the mayor's secretary connected them, Hawkins blurted out in an excited manner, "Mr. Mayor, we have our first solid lead in Chief Macklin's murder."

"What have you got Hawkins? Whatever the fuck it is, it better be good. These motherfuckers from the press have chewed my ass raw because we haven't come up with something."

"What I have sir, I don't want to discuss over the phone. When can we meet?"

"What the fuck do you mean when can we meet? If you have something about the case that will get those blood sucking bastards off of my ass, you should already be halfway here."

Getting off the elevator in the City County Building, Chief Hawkins had barely stepped into the reception area when the mayor's secretary directed him to go on into the office.

"Well Hawkins, what do you have?" the mayor asks impatiently.

Once again, thinking better about pulling out the old briar pipe, Chief Hawkins answers in a cautious manner, "Okay Mr. Mayor, here's what I've learned. The last time that Chief Macklin was at work, he was overheard talking on his cell phone. Now he was heard mentioning the name 'Sharon.' I'm sure you remember she's the officer that was in charge of the evidence room where the drugs were taken from. Now here's the interesting part. Macklin was heard mentioning that Sharon was supposed to pick up some money at the house that his body was found at."

"Who was he talking to?" ask the mayor with a glimmer of hope in his voice.

"At this point we don't know sir. But I was at that house and I can't see where somebody could have hidden any money. Uh, uh. Here's what I think. I think somebody called Macklin and fed him some bullshit about Sharon coming there to get the money. I think that it was somebody that understood Macklin's aggressive, greedy nature . . . somebody that was reasonably sure that if Macklin felt that he could make an arrest all by himself and not have to share the spotlight, he would; in other words, I think that Chief Macklin was set up."

With a look of incredibility on his face, the mayor asks, "Set up, why would somebody want to set up the Chief of Police to be killed? And who would profit by that? It doesn't make sense."

"I don't have the answer to that Mr. Mayor, but I do think that my theory is correct. Nothing else makes sense. Now here's something else that I believe. I believe that whoever made that call to Macklin was somebody from the inside."

"From the inside, inside of what?" questions the Mayor.

"From inside the department sir. Whoever called him, called him on his cell phone. That means it had to be someone that knew him in order to have access to his cell number. If it had been somebody from the outside, they would have called on his office phone. Plus, like I said, it had to be somebody that knew how he operated in order to lure him there." Digesting all that Chief Hawkins had to say, the mayor sits in silence for a few minutes before speaking.

"God damn Hawkins, if what you're saying is true, we're sitting on top of a fucking powder keg. If someone in the Police Department had anything to do with the murder of Chief Macklin, the repercussions are going to be a motherfucker. We can't let the press hear about this shit until we find out if you're right."

"I'll get right on trying to prove my theory sir. I think that the first thing we need to do is get Macklin's cell phone records and see if we can find who made that call to him."

"Yeah, good idea Hawkins, get on it and keep me informed. Oh by the way, did that pain-in-the ass, Captain Lopez move out of the office yet? His people got pissed off because I stopped work on everything else to concentrate on this case. They said it didn't make sense for him to stay here if we're not working on the drug case. I couldn't agree with them more. Fuck them, fuck him and fuck anybody else that want to tell me how to run my fucking city."

"Yes sir Mr. Mayor, he left a little while ago," answered the Chief with a little smile on his face.

Chapter 18

Teaching Young Dawgs New Tricks

Leaving the City County Building, Chief Hawkins feels that for the first time in weeks, things might be taking a change for the better. First thing in the win category for him was getting rid of Captain Lopez, and now it seems as if for the first time, he has a good solid lead into the murder of Chief Macklin . . . and on top of all that, Sharon's name has surfaced again. He has a gut feeling that all of this is connected in some way . . . and something else that keeps eating at the back of his mind, Tonya . . . who in the hell is this Tonya that keeps popping up? Drawing from years of experience as cop, he knows that it's too much of a coincidence for a name to keep coming up unless there's a reason for it. He knows that his job is to find out what that reason is, and he knows just where to start.

Turning the unmarked Dodge onto the Lodge Freeway, he takes it northbound to I-94, and then he takes I-94 to the Westside and comes up at the Warren Street exit. Traveling down Warren, he comes to a stop in front of the G.M.O. Club (Gang Member's Only).

Entering the building, he notice's a stark difference from the last time that he was here a few weeks ago. Before, the vestibule was brightly lit, now there is only one light fixture operating to light the hallway. When he was here before, there was somebody stationed at the inside entrance to check him into the recreation area, now the door was abandoned and stood open.

Reaching beneath his coat, his hand comes to rest on the handle of his service revolver as he makes his way into the dimly lit gymnasium. Once inside, he notices that the place is empty. He cautiously approaches the office where he sees a light burning. Peeping inside, he removes his hand from his gun and enters.

Startled at the sound of the office door being opened, Jasper jerks his head around in surprise. "Damn Captain, what you trying to do? Give a nigga a heart attack."

"Naw Jasper, you're stronger than that," replies Hawkins taking out his old briar pipe and sticking it in his mouth. Making his way over to the sofa and taking a seat, he inquires, "What happened to this place? The last time I was here, there was standing room only, now it looks like a ghost town. What's up?"

With an astonished look on his face, Jasper gets up from his desk and paces back and forth across the room. Speaking in a voice that is about two octaves higher than his normal speaking voice he asks, "What's up? Let me get this straight. You, a cop, come in here and ask me *what's up*." Throwing his hands up into the air in a hopeless gesture and rolling his eyes around in his head, he continues, "I don't believe this shit. Man where you been? Don't you know what's going on in this city?

For a minute, Chief Hawkins sits there dumbfounded. Not being able to understand what Jasper is talking about, he takes his pipe from his mouth and interrupts him, "Whoa Jasper, slow down. What the hell are you hollering about? Maybe if you cut out some of the drama and tell me what you're talking about, I could understand what you're trying to say."

Still in a high-pitched voice, Jasper tries to explain as he continues to pace the floor. "Cops man, I'm talking 'bout cops. In case you don't know it, cops don' shut this city down. Look at this place, wanna know why ain't one nigga in here? Fo' 'bout a month now, every nigga that walk the street, don' either got his head busted or been hassled by the cops. And it ain't just in here. It's all over the city. This city be like a ghost town. Nigga's scared to come up fo' air."

As understanding of what Jasper is saying began to seep into his skull, Hawkins places the pipe back into his mouth and goes silent for a while. Yes he knew what had been happening on the streets of Detroit, but only from a cop's perspective. He never gave a thought to what price the innocent citizens of the city were paying. While it was true that the crime rate had took a drastic drop, how many decent, innocent people had paid for it in terms of being harassed unnecessarily, had been bullied and even beaten. And what about this place? A club that he himself had been instrumental in starting, and was now being destroyed because of police having unrestricted, free reign over the city. The more he thought about it, the more he could understand why Jasper was in an uproar.

Blowing a puff of smoke into the air, Hawkins finally breaks the silence. "All I can say at this point Jasper, is I'm sorry. I know that saying I'm sorry don't mean a lot. But right now, that's all I have. Just like you want me to have understanding about your problems, I would like for you to have some understanding about mine. A police chief has been murdered in this city and God himself can't stop the powers that be, from doing whatever it takes to find the killer. Now I know that you can understand that, because if we don't, every cop in this town might as well have a bulls eye painted on his chest, because it's going to be open warfare on us. And that, we can't afford."

"I'm not saying it's okay to kill a cop," retorted Jasper, "But you saying it's okay to fuck nigga's up cause a cop got killed?"

"You know that's not what I'm saying Jasper, and look. Do me a favor. Why don't you bury that word . . . nigga? I know you and I can talk together better than that."

Managing a slight smile, Jasper chuckles, "Ha, ha, ha. This is something. With all the shit that be going on, here's a white man that's pissed cause a black man says the word 'nigga.' Well I guess we don' finally overcome. Yeah captain, I can understand why ya'll want to catch yawls killer, but there's got to be a better way to do it."

"I'm glad you said that Jasper, as a matter of fact that's why I came over today. There's a name that keeps popping up . . . Tonya. I need to know everything that you can tell me about her."

Stopping his pacing long enough to take a seat at his desk, Jasper lets out a long breath of air. "I told you 'bout her. I said she was Rico's woman."

"Yes, yes I know," prompted Hawkins, "But I need to know everything about her that you can tell me."

"Well let's see," says Jasper scratching his head, "Tonya, Tonya, okay, here goes . . . Far as I can remember, Tonya first started coming around when she was 'bout fo'teen, maybe fifteen years old. She lived on the Eastside, but fo' some strange reason, she liked to hang out on the Westside with us . . . matter of fact, her uncle Gator was the leader of the Satan's Disciples, who was our rivals.

Anyway, like I said, she hung out with us all the time. Sometimes she would bring other bitches with her, and me and Rico would get them high and fuck the shit out of 'em which was okay cause that's what they came fo'. Everything was cool til' Rico got a nose job over her. Now I didn't notice anything foul at first, cause I was fuckin' her bout much as he was, but to me, it was just pussy. And I think that's all it was to her, cause it didn't matter if it was pussy or a dick, she just loved to fuck. But after awhile, I started to notice how she could make Rico do just about anything she wanted him to.

I'm no hater, if my main man was in love . . . hey, good for him, so I didn't pay too much attention to it. But after all that shit went down, I found out just how smart that Ho' really is. So all I can tell you is this, if she be involved in yo' case, you better keep yo' back to the wall. She is a treacherous, freaky, low-life bitch, but she be smart as they come."

"What about her family? Do you think they might be hiding her somewhere?"

"Man, you got to be kidding? All her people are crackheads, they would flip a dime on her ass in a Hong Kong second fo' a rock."

"What about out of town? Do you know if she has people in other states?" prodded Hawkins.

"If she do, I ain't heard about it," replied Jasper. And added as an afterthought, "But what do Tonya have to do with a cop getting killed?"

"I don't know! Maybe nothing, like I said before, for some reason her name just keeps popping up."

"Alright captain, now that I don' told you everything I know, what you gon' do about the streets? I want to get this place alive again."

"Jasper I've got an idea. You keep calling me captain . . . let me make a correction, I'm not a captain anymore, I'm the new Chief of Police. I'm telling you that, to ask you this. Have you ever thought about becoming a police officer?"

Jasper is left speechless. His jaw drops as his mouth is left wide open, looking at Hawkins with disbelief, he finally screams out a word, "WHAT, are you out of yo' fuckin' mind?! Hell naw, I ain't never thought no shit like that. Why you ask me some bullshit like that anyway?"

Smiling, Chief Hawkins answers, "That's just the reaction that I thought I would get. But before you dismiss the idea completely, listen to me for a minute." Relighting his old briar pipe, Hawkins sat on the edge of the sofa facing Jasper looking him eye to eye. "For some reason our paths seem to be intertwined, starting with you saving my life. In the situation that you were in, you didn't have to do that, but you did and I'm grateful. But it goes much farther than that. I gave you a chance to help the kids of this city and look what you've done . . . through this place you've worked miracles. And believe me when I say, it will be back open. As chief of police, I can promise you that. Jasper, I have a feeling that you are meant for greatness. I think that this club is only the beginning of what you can do for this city. As a private citizen, you are limited to what you can accomplish, but as member of law enforcement, you'll have the tools necessary to do greater things. As I said before Jasper, you'll have the best of experience from both worlds, legal and illegal. What do you say?"

"What do I say? I say you're nuts. Me a cop! Man, that's a good one. And you of all people, Captain . . . Chief, whatever you is. You know what kind of life I've lead, I'm a gangster, a hustler, a hood rat. What kind of cop would I make?"

"The best kind Jasper, someone that has been there, someone that will know what it's like on both sides. Just like you opened my eyes to what's happening in the city now, I only saw it from a cop's perspective, but you reminded me that every coin has two sides and both sides have to be taken into consideration. Jasper, you're a natural for this."

Back to pacing the floor again, Jaspers mind is a whirling dervish as Chief Hawkins words burrows deep into his brain.

"Man I been hustling and selling dope in this city all my life, ain't no way in hell they gon' let me be a cop . . . naw, that's just crazy thinking."

"Wait a minute Jasper, it might not be as crazy as you think. Yes I'm aware of what you've done in your past, but here's something that I bet you've never considered; you have no record. I've already checked and there is no police record on file for Roy White."

Stopping in his tracks, Jasper looks at Hawkins with an odd expression on his face. "Damn Chief, that's right. I don' did so much foul shit in this city, I forgot I ain't never been arrested." But just as suddenly as a smile was beginning to creep across his face, it disappeared. "Yeah well, all that might be swell and good, but there's one thing that I bet you didn't think about. If you did your checking, I'm sure you found out I didn't finish school, and I know you got to be don' finished school to be a cop."

Blowing a puff of smoke into the air, Chief Hawkins let it dissipate before he replies, "Yes, you're absolutely right. One of the requirements for becoming a police officer is graduation from high school. And yes I did check, and yes, I know that you didn't finish school, but I don't think that will present a problem. You see, I also checked your elementary and middle school records that you had before you dropped out, and guess what . . . you had all a's and b's. So I don't think passing a GED test will be a problem. Any other excuses?"

Going back to sit at his desk, Jasper can hardly think straight. "You went to all that trouble checking me out, why?"

"Because like I said Jasper, I believe that you're meant for great things, and I believe in you. But I can only offer you the chance, it's up to you to take it. I believe a young dog can learn new tricks."

"I hear what you be saying Chief, but I've got a lot of things to think about. I can't give you my answer right now, but I will think about it and let you know, okay?"

"That's good enough for right now Jasper, but I will be waiting to hear from you. In the meantime I'm going to get to work on easing things up on the streets a little, so people won't have to be afraid to come out of their houses. So I'll see you later . . . and like I said, I'll be waiting for your call."

A S A   P u b l i s h i n g   C o m p a n y

Chapter 19

Solemn Vow

A couple of weeks later, Chief Hawkins finds himself once again in the mayor's office. Mayor William's is in a particularly foul mood as he sits at his massive desk reading over the reports that Hawkins had brought with him. Glancing up at Hawkins, he slams his fist down on his desk so hard, that the folder's that were sitting there; fly off the desk and land on the floor.

"God damn it Hawkins, what the fuck is this bullshit?" shout's the mayor at the top of his lungs, "You have the fucking nerve to sit here in my god damn office and tell me, this is all you have? After three months of investigations, you bring me this little weak ass report that don't mean jack shit."

He emphasizes his point by throwing the report at Hawkins. "You can take this shit and stick it up your ass. Do you have any fucking idea how much taxpayer's money we've spent on these goddamn cases? Well I'll tell you . . . plenty. And all we've got to show for it is a stack of fucking papers that don't mean shit. I've given you permission to shut this fucking city down. I've given you permission to put all the other police matters on hold, until this murder case has been solved. And what do I get? Reports . . . not one motherfucking arrest! All I get is motherfucking reports. Do you have any Idea what I've had to go through with those assholes on the city council? Well let me tell you my friend, it hasn't been pretty. They would like to take my goddamn nuts and put them in a blender, and these fucking reports sure aren't helping to keep them out.

I took plenty of heat from the Feds when they too had pulled that son-of-bitch Lopez off the drug case because we wasn't working it, I didn't mind that because catching Macklin's killer was more important. But it is only important if we get results, but all I get is fucking reports."

Finally with some of the steam leaving him, Mayor William let out a gulp of air and leans back on his chair, puts his elbow on the desk and props his hand under his chin. With a milder manner and lower tone, he continues, "Look man, I don't mean to sound like I'm holding you personally responsible for this shit. I know that you're a fine officer, and have been for a lot of years. But you have to appreciate the position that I'm in. As mayor of this city, everything starts and stops with me. I'm held responsible for every fucking thing. From the cracks in the sidewalks, to how much rain we get. I'm not complaining, it comes with the job. I'm just telling you how much pressure I'm under on a normal basis, pressure I don't mind as long as I can produce results. But when my ass is on the chopping block, and all I can produce is reports . . . understand where I'm coming from?"

Sitting in silence all through the mayor's tirade, Chief Hawkins emotions runs the scale, from anger at being verbally attacked, to empathy for the mayor having been placed in such a pressure packed situation.

Out of habit and not giving consideration to where he was, he puts his old briar pipe in his mouth and lights it. Speaking with the pipe clenched between his teeth, he addresses the mayor, "Mr. Mayor, believe me, there's no one that would like to find out who killed Chief Macklin any more than I would. And believe me, everything that can be done, is being done. Those reports are the results of a lot of good men and women dedicating themselves to that task. They have been working non-stop, sixteen to eighteen hour days, seven days a week to solve this case. We have turned this city upside down and inside out. Everything that has been said, talked about, whispered about, seen or even though about pertaining to the murder, is in that report . . . so you have to excuse me if I can't agree with you when you say *just a fucking report.*"

More than a little amazed at Chief Hawkins standing up to him, the mayor is secretly pleased that he is showing some spunk. With a slight grin on his face, he replies, "Yeah, yeah, yeah Hawkins, I know that you and your people have been working hard, but like I said, results are what counts, and up until now, we have no fucking results."

"That's not exactly true sir," objects Hawkins, "I admit that we haven't made an arrest yet, but when you read through those reports, I'm sure that you'll agree that we are miles ahead from where we started. First of all, we have learned for a fact that the missing drugs and Chief Macklin's murder are connected. We know this because it's been pretty much proven that Officer Sharon Morgan is responsible for the missing drugs, so it's not hard to believe that is not a coincidence that her name popped up in the murder investigation, all we have to do is figure out how they are tied together.

Furthermore, through our investigations, all of the evidence that we have gathered, points to the fact that Macklin's murder was an inside job, somebody in this department wanted him dead. When we find out why, I'm sure we'll find out who! Mr. Mayor, I'm making you a solemn promise, if it takes me until my last day on this earth, I'm going to find the answer to these questions."

Mayor Williams stares at Hawkins with a look of newfound respect. Nodding his head in agreement, he reaches out his hand to be shaken. "I like your attitude Hawkins, I think

I made the right choice when I appointed you as Police Chief. Now in the meantime, we have to get this city back to normal as much as we can. I want you to keep a special task force working on Macklin's case, but I also want you to let your people go back to whatever cases that they were working on before, I still have a city to run and I can't afford to keep it shut down any longer."

Getting up from his seat, Chief Hawkins heads for the door. Just as he reaches it to go out, Mayor Williams calls out to him, "Oh by the way Hawkins, the next time you pull out that old god damn pipe in my office, I'm going to break my foot off in your fucking ass," he says with a grin.

Chapter 20

Back to the Future

Turning the hot steamy water off, and stepping out of the shower, Tonya takes a soft fluffy towel from the towel rack, places it around her neck, and walks over to the bed where Sharon has been reliving memories of by gone days. Playfully throwing the towel at her, she startles her back to the present.

"Damn baby, that oohh-weee . . . don' got yo' ass fucked up, I ain't heard a word out of yo' ass since I been in the shower."

Standing there with her legs slightly apart, she bends over and pushes her ass towards Sharon's face. With a sultry whine, she asks, "Do you mind taking that towel and drying me off?" Finally coming back from her trip down memory lane, Sharon takes the towel, and began to gently rub it against Tonya's smooth black skin. After drying Tonya's ass, she stands up from the bed and turns her around to face her. Starting with her neck, she rubs the towel across her shoulders, making just enough contact with her skin, for the towel to absorb the water. Next she moves the towel to Tonya's full, firm succulent tits. Massaging them with the towel until the nipples began to harden, she then moves on down to her soft, flat stomach. Sitting back down on the bed, Sharon rubs the towel, first up and down one leg, and then up and down the other.

Tonya, feeling the sensual exhilaration from the towel massage, is a little perplexed at the sudden cessation, as Sharon puts the towel down. "Wow honey, why you got to stop now? You ain't through drying me off yet. My kitty cat is still soaking wet. What you gon' do 'bout her?"

"Don't worry about that my love. Delicate things call for delicate handling," Sharon replies with a wink.

Still in a sitting position, she picks one of Tonya's legs up and places it across her shoulder. With a hand on each cheek of her ass, she pulls her forward until she makes contact with her stomach. Trailing her tongue from the navel, to the forest of bushy hair between her legs, she takes her tongue and pushes the hair aside so that she can get at the pea size clit that is hiding there. Taking the clit between her lips, she alternates between sucking on it, and gently massaging it with her tongue until it becomes hard as a rock.

Soft moaning noises began to build up in Tonya's throat, as she is enjoying the tongue-lashing. Shifting gears, Sharon stabs her tongue into the deep, sweet recesses of her pussy. She stabs it in and out with piston like precision until the soft moaning noises that was in Tonya's throat, has now turned into an ear piercing scream. "Eeeeiiihhhh, oh my god, please don't stopppppp."

Under the assault of Sharon's tongue, thoughts ran through Tonya's mind. Thoughts of defying the laws of possibilities . . . she was sure that if she could figure out just the right angle, she could figure out how to stuff Sharon's entire head all the way into her pussy. She knew the answer to the mystery was right there . . . if only she could stop screaming long enough. But the more she screamed, the faster Sharon worked her tongue in and out of her pussy until finally with her whole body bucking and shaking, she let out with one last earth shattering scream. "Ooooooohhhhh, myyyyyyyy, god. That's sooooo dammmm, gooooooooood."

As wave after wave of orgasmic pleasure washed through her body, Sharon held her glued tightly too her face with her tongue sunk deeply into her pussy lapping up every single drop of the intoxicating love juice. Finally with Tonya's body going limp as a dishrag, Sharon detaches her tongue from her pussy, and gently lays her across the bed. All that Tonya can manage to do is lay there in a fetal position and moan.

"Mmmmmmmmmm, oh my god, baby that was unbelievable, oooooooommmmm . . . let me rest for just a minute, then we gotta go, we're already late, and you know we don't want to make Chavez wait.

Understanding the importance of what Tonya is saying, Sharon reluctantly agrees. Putting a little hurt into her voice, she replies, "Alright love, I know that we have business to take care of, so let's go do what we gotta do, but remember . . . you owe me."

Putting her arm around Sharon's neck and pulling her down to meet her mouth, she engages her in a long passionate kiss. "Sweetheart, you know me well enough to know I always pay my bills, and that's one bill I'm gonna pay with interest."

After dressing in a white silk sundress that was form fitting at the top, (with a plunging neckline that showed off her magnificent breast) and with a flared out bottom that stopped four inches above her knees to display her gorgeous, long shapely legs. She accented the outfit with a pair of four inch, white strapless heels, which made her look even taller than her five foot, ten inch height. Adorning her head with a White Felt wide brim hat, she grabbed a matching white beaded purse to complete her ensemble. With all of that white to accent her smooth black skin, she was a visual delight. Turning around in a modeling pose, she looks to Sharon for approval. "Well baby, how do I look?"

"How do you look? Shiiiiit. You look good enough to eat," replies Sharon jokingly as she reaches for her.

Jumping back beyond her reach, Tonya giggles, "Oh no you don't. If we start that again, we ain't gon' never get otta here."

Exiting the elevator, the two women walk with a provocative switch in their step. It was amusing to see the approving looks of the men that were watching their asses as they seesawed back and forth in the outfits that they were wearing. It wasn't just the men, they noticed several women that were taking more than just a passing interest in them also. And the women that wasn't having secret thoughts of pleasure . . . you could see, had hater written all over them.

Stepping on through the lobby of the hotel to the entrance, they saw that the Bellman had brought Tonya's car around as ordered. As they approached the white on white Mercedes Benz, the Bellman opened the door for Sharon. Going around to the driver's side, he opened the door for Tonya to get in. As she slid onto the soft white leather seat, she purposely let the bottom of her dress ride high enough up her thigh to expose the crouch of the red bikini panties that she was wearing. Holding out a ten dollar tip, she had to practically shove it into his hand in order for him to tear his eyes away from her legs to notice it. Embarrassed that he had got caught stealing a peep, the flushed face man utters a shaky . . . "Thank you mam."

Expertly handling the Benz, Tonya enters the freeway and takes Interstate-5 towards Century City. After they have been traveling about twenty minutes, Sharon breaks the silence. "Why did you play that number on that poor guy?"

Caught off guard at the question, Tonya asks, "What number on what guy?"

"Oh come on Tonya, you know exactly what I'm talking about. You practically had that poor Bellman about to nut in his pants."

Busting out in giggle, Tonya replies, "Hee, hee, hee, hee. Oh that! You got to understand the whole story 'bout that . . . That's Justin. Ever since I been staying there, that white boy don' did everything but beg fo' some of this pussy. Any time I call down to the desk fo' somethin', he make sho' he brings it personally. One day I called down to maid service fo' some towels, well he heard about it and next thing I know, here he comes wit' em. Now maid service ain't nowhere in his job description . . . so that's when I started to fuck wit' him. When I saw it was him at the do', I said just a minute, I took off all my clothes and put on my robe. When I let him in, he couldn't hardly hand me the towels fo' looking at me. He handed me the towels and backed out the do'. I had tied my robe real loose . . . as I started walking towards him, it fell open, and all my shit was there to be seen. That white boy turned red as a fucking beet, I think he was otta that do' and down the hall in 'bout two steps. I just about bust a gut laughing at that muthafucka', and I been fuckin' wit' him ever since."

"Yeah baby, that's some funny shit alright, but I want you to be careful. Everybody's not to be fucked with, and I don't want to have to go gorilla on somebody's ass for fucking with you."

"I know you be right baby, and believe me I'm careful. Besides, you know I can handle myself, so don't worry. Tell you what, I know you haven't had no sleep and we still got a long way to go, why don't you let yo' seat back and take a nap till we get there, I need you to be real sharp."

Nodding in agreement, Sharon reclines the seat of the Benz, and gets comfortable. As the soft music coming from the CD player combines with her exhaustion, sleep begins to overpower her consciousness, and as it does, once again her mind travel back to five years ago . . . back to when they had just left Detroit.

Chapter 21

Two for the road

Leaving the Detroit Metropolitan Airport, Tonya and Sharon sat in silence as they head west on Interstate I-94, leading out of town. Not having any idea of where they were going, neither wanted to speak for fear of letting the other one know how scared they really were. Finally breaking the silence, Tonya starts to talk, as she expertly guides the car through the night.

"Well baby, so far so good," she says, trying to put a little bravado in her voice, "Do you think that little trick that we pulled will fool 'em?"

Trying to put on a brave front, Sharon replies, "Yeah, I'm pretty sure. By the time they exhaust all of their leads at the airport, we'll have time to get to anywhere we want to go. By the way, where do we want to go?"

"I don't know. Right now, I just want to put as much distance between me and Detroit as I can."

With a look of amazement on her face, Sharon screams in a high-pitched voice, "You don't know! You mean to tell me we're out here driving around in the fucking dark, and you don't have any idea where in the hell we're going?"

Fear mixed with anger, prompt's Tonya to fire right back at her. Shouting at the top of her lungs, she screams.

"Wait just a god damn minute bitch! It ain't like I had time to plan this little vacation. As a matter of fact, you wasn't even invited . . . you invited yo' self. And I'll tell you something else, you be the one that's hot as hell, not me! Yeah I know Jasper might be looking fo' me, but that's a damn sight better than what you got . . . you gon' have every fuckin' cop in America looking fo' yo' ass. Now here's dumb ass me, hooking up with you. The only thing that will do, is bring yo' heat down on my black ass, and this is all the thanks I get fo' helping a muthafucka out?"

As the sting of Tonya's words hit home, Sharon realizes that she is right. She had been so caught up in her own problems, that she didn't take the time to realize what a burden that Tonya was placing on herself just by having her with her. Finally realizing what a predicament that she was really in, tears started to flow down her cheeks.

"I'm sorry Tonya," she mutters through trembling lips, "You're right about everything. I didn't mean to come apart on you like that, it's just that I'm so scared. And I want you to know that I do appreciate what you're doing for me."

Glancing at the tears coming down Sharon's face, Tonya has a rare moment of tenderness come over her. In a low compassionate tone, she finds herself consoling her.

"I know baby, I know. Look, I'm sorry too. I didn't mean to put all the weight on you. Like I told you befo', the only way we gon' make this shit work, is to work together. Now come on and dry yo' eye's befo' you start me to crying."

Wiping her eyes and trying to pull herself together, she confesses in a shaky voice. "I'm sorry for being so weak like this, but it'll pass. Just stick with me baby. You can trust me to have your back all the way."

"Now you be talking like my girl," replies Tonya.

Glad that she had shown a little understanding, because admit it or not, she was scared shitless herself, and it felt a damn sight better to have somebody with her, than to be out here all by herself. She had said that the only one she had to worry about looking for her was Jasper. But in truth, she wasn't sure. She didn't know whether or not the police were also looking for her. She knew that she had wiped Rico's house as clean of her fingerprints as she could. But she realized that the house was a murder scene, so she had to figure that the police, with all of their scientific equipment, was not going to leave a stone unturned. So who knows what they may have found to connect her ass with it. No, she couldn't afford to take the slightest chance, and get caught by doing some silly shit. And she knew that by Sharon being a cop for all those years, she was her best chance of staying free. She figured that if she could keep Sharon calm, and use her knowledge of police procedures, they would both stand a better chance of keeping their asses out of prison.

Seeing that Sharon was calming down, she decided that now was a good time to start picking her brain. "Listen baby, I want you to put on yo' thinking cap. If you was on the job, and you was chasing a couple of bad ass bitches like us, what kind of mistakes would you be looking fo' them to make?

With her tears wiped dry, and her emotions under complete control, Sharon's mind goes into police mode. "Uuuummmm, if we were looking for somebody that was on the run, there are a few things that we would automatically do. First we would check with all of your relatives, in and out of town. Then we would check with all of your known friends. If you had a checking account, we could find out where was the last place you wrote one. If you have a credit card and used it, we could find out, when and where."

"Damn, the cops got all that shit going fo' 'em . . . how is a nigga gon' get away with all that shit against 'em."

With her knowledge of how the police work, Sharon finally began to feel like she is contributing something. As a matter of fact, she start's to feel like she has a little power. After all, she is not only the older of the two, she is the one with all the formal training, so it seemed only natural that she take more of a leadership role. With her new found strength, she answer's with a smugness to her voice. "Now hold on sweetness, I didn't say that cops were the smartest motherfuckers in the world. Sure they have a lot of tools to work with, but to tell the truth . . . they also get a lot of luck in solving cases, most of the time it's through the criminal's own carelessness or stupidity, whichever one you want to call it. Now I'm not saying that they are the stupidest people in the world either, they got some people that really know their shit. What I am saying is, that if we be careful, and eliminate silly mistakes, we stand a better chance of staying free, than they do of finding us."

Hearing these words of encouragement, Tonya's hopes of eluding capture were placed on a higher level. Plus, just the fact that Sharon was adding something positive to their situation, helped to take some of the burden of thinking for the both of them, off of her.

"Yeah, I see what you're saying Sharon, and it makes sense. When you see them suckers get jammed on the six o'clock news, it be because after they hit a lick, they go running their mouths off and somebody drop a dime on their ass. You right, all we got to do is be cool and everything will be alright."

"Like I said, all we have to do is make sure we eliminate the stupid mistakes, and we are home free. I suggest the first thing that we do is get rid of all of our credit cards and check books so we don't be tempted to use them. As soon as we stop for the night, we should cut them up and flush them down the toilet. Anything that we need, we'll pay cash it . . . cash don't leave no trail. Speaking of stopping for the night, we've been driving for five or six hours. I think we should find a motel, get us something to eat, and get us a good night's sleep."

The suggestion of stopping for the night and getting something to eat, makes Tonya realize how tired and hungry she is. A mile later she spots a sign that says, "Food and Lodging, Next Exit". After getting off of the freeway and following a sign that indicates; restaurant, she pulls into the parking lot and turns the motor off. Yawning and stretching her arms over her head, she calls out to Sharon, "Come on baby, let's go get our grub on."

"Whoa Tonya, Wait a minute, remember what I said about not making stupid mistakes? Think for a second. The police might not be looking for you, but you can bet your sweet ass they're looking for me. By now they probably have my name and picture plastered all over the TV and newspapers. Right now we have the advantage because they don't know which way we're headed, but all we need is for somebody to recognize my face and drop a dime on my ass and we're through. So you go on in and get us some carryout, we'll find a motel and eat there."

After checking into the motel, Tonya comes back out with the key. Getting back into the car, she pulls around to the back of the building and parks.

"I took this room on the back 'cause I figure there'll be less traffic. Now come on, let's go in and eat, I'm hungrier than a mutha'."

Once settled in the room, both women attack the food like hungry lion's. After their appetite's has been satisfied, Tonya heads for the shower while Sharon lays back and relaxes on the bed drifting off to sleep. After a while she is nudged awake.

"Okay girl, just like a nigga, soon as you eat . . . you wanna go to sleep. Wake yo' ass up, I left the water running fo' you and it's nice and hot. Go on and wash that road funk off of yo' ass."

Opening her sleep laden eye's, Sharon looks up at Tonya sitting there stark naked. No matter how many times she has seen her like this, she still has a hard time tearing her eyes away from her body. Regardless of how hard she tries, she can't control her hand as it creeps upon Tonya's thigh and dips between them to run her fingers through the long coarse hair that guards the entrance to her pussy.

"Come on baby," moans Tonya. "Don't do me like this, go on and take yo' shower befo' the water get cold, I'm tired and I know you are too. This ole' pussy ain't going nowhere, it's yours fo' life . . . but right now, we need some sleep." Reluctantly, Sharon removes her hand and starts for the bathroom. Looking back over her shoulder, she adds light heartedly.

"Huh, who said anything about me wanting your ole' pussy for the rest of my life?"

Chapter 22

The best laid plans

The sound of birds chirping mixed with the sunlight that filtered through the window blinds, stirred Tonya from an exhausted sleep. Rubbing the sleep from her eyes, she feels totally comfortable and at ease as she enjoys the contact of Sharon's naked body pressed up against hers. Turning her head slightly to the side, she gently blows a stream of warm air into her ear causing Sharon to stir and press herself even closer to her. Wrapping her arms around her, feelings of tenderness washes over her as she plants tiny kisses on Sharon's forehead and neck. She whispers.

"Wake up sleepyhead, you plan on sleeping all day?"

Responding to the kissing, Sharon snuggles in Tonya's arms and yarns. "Good morning love. I guess I was more tired than I thought."

"Yeah, me too. But now we gotta get our asses in gear and get on down the road."

Disengaging herself from Tonya, and sitting upon the side of the bed, Sharon stretches her arms out and yarns.

"Wait a minute baby, let's take time to think. So far we haven't had time to make any plans, we've just been going on instinct. So far, so good, but we can't rely on just being lucky. We have to know what we're going to do before we do it."

Beginning to get a little pissed off at Sharon's overly cautious ways, Tonya retorts, "Damn Sharon, you beginning to sound like some mother hen or somethin', we been doing alright so far, why don't we just get the fuck otta here and keep going?"

"Yeah Tonya, we can do that . . . but go where? We're not ready yet. Without a plan, we're lucky if we're not in jail before nightfall. Take for instance, clothes. All I saw you bring in was that pillowcase. So my guess is, even though you have a clean ass, you don't even have a pair of clean draws to put on it."

"So fucking what! We can stop anywhere and buy clothes," barks Tonya."

"Okay, say we do stop somewhere and by clothes, what do I do while you're in the store shopping . . . stay in the car? That's just great, somebody spots me sitting there and then what? And another thing; we need to do something about that money and dope that you have in that pillowcase."

At the sound of Sharon mentioning the contents of the pillowcase, Tonya asks suspiciously.

"What do you mean we need to do something about it?"

"Just that. We need to do something about it. You look awful suspicious carrying a pillowcase around with you everywhere you go. Remember what I said about making simple mistakes? Well, that could be the one to get us caught."

Sheepishly, Tonya had to admit what Sharon saying made sense.

"You right again baby. I guess I ain't cut out for thinkin' like the police. Maybe I better leave that to you. So what you think we should do next?"

"Alright, here's what you do. First, you take some money from your pillowcase to do your shopping; all small bills, nothing larger that twenty's and not over two or three hundred dollars' worth. Go to a K-Mart or Target, nothing upscale. These kind of stores see so many nigga's every day, they couldn't tell one from the other. Buy you enough outfits to last three or four days . . . nothing fancy, just plain shit. Also buy a medium size suitcase. Then I want you to find a wig shop, buy me a medium length wig . . . make sure it's brown . . . don't get nothing with streaks or anything fancy. Next go to a CVS and get a bottle of liquid bandage, and last of all, stop at a drive-thru restaurant and get us some breakfast."

"Damn bitch, that's a fuckin' grocery list. Why we need all that shit?"

Reaching over to playfully slap her on her naked ass, Sharon replies, "Didn't you just get through saying that you're going to leave the thinking to me? I'll explain it all to you when you get back."

Chapter 23

Running on empty

The sharp knock on the door startles Sharon from a light sleep. Not bothering to put on any clothes, she gets up from the bed and looks through the peephole. Recognizing Tonya standing there loaded down with bags, she position's herself behind the door so as not to be seen, and opens it.

"Damn girl, help me with some of this shit," cries Tonya, handing some of the bags to Sharon. Coming into the room, she lays the rest of them on the bed and takes a seat. "I'm tired as a muthafucka. I still don't see why we need all this shit."

Surveying the bags, Sharon asks, "Did you get everything?"

"Yeah, I got everything that you asked fo'. I know what the food and clothes be fo' . . . to eat and cover my ass with. But why all the strange instructions 'bout all the other shit. What that be 'bout?"

"Okay sugar, it's pretty simple, but let me explain it to you. The last thing that we want to do is attract unwanted attention, so that's why I told you not to take any bills larger than a twenty, and not over three hundred dollars' worth. As far as what store to shop at, K-Mart and Target cashiers see nigga's coming and going all day long, so as long as you don't spend too much money and make an impression on somebody, even if someone showed them a picture of you, it's highly unlikely that they'll remember you from anybody else. Now for the wig . . . people have a tendency to notice things that are done to the extreme. For instance long or short hair, that's why I said get me a medium length wig, one with no streaks or fancy style. Just an everyday plain one that won't attract attention. Last of all, the Plastic Bandage. Wherever we go it's going to be impossible for me not to touch something. That stuff is a temporary cure all. With that sprayed on your fingertips . . . it solidifies and cover's your fingerprints. Does that answer all your questions?" Sharon ends with a smile.

"Goddamn baby," squeals Tonya, with respect in her voice. "You mean to tell me that you don' thought that far ahead . . . see, that's what I'm talking 'bout. With both of our brains together, can't nobody fuck with us."

Reveling in the adulation, Sharon reaches for the bag of food. "It's like I said, the main things that we have to avoid is making simple stupid mistakes. If we do that we stand a pretty good chance of staying free."

An hour later, after they had finished their breakfast, Tonya changes into one of the new outfits that she had bought, while Sharon dresses and places the new wig on her head. After looking at herself in the mirror, Tonya squenches her face up as if she had smelled something nasty.

"Oh hell naw Sharon, I know you ain't expecting me to wear this shit, no way in the fuck," cried Tonya, referring to the K-Mart outfit she had just put on. Looking at her standing in front of the mirror, dressed in the loose fitting jeans and oversized shirt, Sharon worked hard to suppress the laugh that was trying to creep up her throat. Instead she said words of encouragement.

"Look honey, I know that's not the kind of designer outfits that you're used to wearing but like I said, we don't want to draw any attention. And with that fine ass body of yours, all you have to do is stuff it into something tight and anybody that see you is going to remember. I know that what you're wearing is not to your liking, but I guarantee you, it looks a hell of a lot better than prison stripes."

"Yeah, when you put it that way, I guess you're right," responded Tonya.

"I guess we have to do what we have to do, come on let's get the fuck up outta here."

Ten minutes later, Tonya has checked them out of the Motel and once again they are on the expressway. Going around the Chicago loop, they pick up I-40 traveling Westbound, heading towards St. Louis, MO. Being careful to keep the car just under the speed limit, Sharon constantly checks her rear and side view mirrors for cops. With the hypnotic effect of the road along with the effect of Tonya's hand that is resting on her thigh, Sharon's mind although cautious, is in a peaceful place as she guides the car down the highway. Her calm is disturbed as Tonya, who has had to call her name several times, finally gets her attention.

"Say baby, I know we ain't discussed where yet, but where do you think we should go?"

Without thinking, Sharon blurted, "California."

"California," repeated Tonya with disbelief in her voice. To her, California was some place that she only saw in the movies or read about in books. She was born and raised in Detroit and the farthest away that she had ever been from there was Ohio when she went to Cedar Point Amusement Park. When she thought of California, she thought of powerful gangs like the Bloods or the Crips. Now faced with even the possibility of going to California; once again it triggered a fear of the unknown.

"Why California baby? I don't know nobody out there. Do you?"

"And that's my point Tonya. We don't know anybody out there, so the police won't have any reason to look for us out there."

Once again, Tonya had to admire her way of thinking.

"Yeah, that's right, I never thought about it like that. Man am I glad you be with me and not against me."

With a little of the fear leaving her, she let her hand creep up Sharon's thigh and under the skirt that she is wearing, until it comes to rest on the thin panties that is covering her pussy. With nimble fingers she moves the panties aside and with a circular motion, she began to message the fluffy mound of hair. After a few minutes a sensation of pleasure began to build up inside of her as Tonya's educated fingers go about their work.

"Awh come on baby," moaned Sharon. "You know this shit isn't fair."

But By now Tonya's fingers have found the Clit that is nestled under the hair and she directs her full attention to it. It takes all of Sharon's driving skills to keep the car under control as she unconsciously spreads her legs as wide as the skirt would allow. With added access to her treasure box, Tonya slips her finger into the hot, wet pussy. With each thrust of Tonya's finger, Sharon roll's her hip's forward to meet it. With Tonya's finger pumping furiously in and out of her pussy, Sharon grips the steering wheel so tight that her knuckles began to turn white as the volcano inside of her erupts.

"Ooooohhhh . . . godddddd . . . daaaammmmn . . . here it coooommmmes, ooooohh, baby pppllleeeaaaassseee," cries Sharon, as wave after wave of pure pleasure washes over her. Finally after Tonya has removed her finger and her body has stopped quivering, Sharon musters up enough strength to speak.

"You are one dirty bitch," says Sharon with mock anger in her voice. "That was dangerous, what if you had made us wreck? But I'll tell you one thing . . . I hope you know payback when you see it."

"Yeah, not only do I know it when I see it . . . I know it when I feel and taste it too," says a teasing Tonya as takes the finger that is still wet with Sharon's love juice and sticks it into her mouth. Wrapping her tongue around it, she sucks it until it is dry of the nectar.

With a smile on her face, Sharon replies, "Alright missy, but remember what I said. We will be stopping for the night, and then it'll be my turn to see just how bad your bad ass really is. But right now I need to stop somewhere and wash up and change out of these wet draws."

"Why don't we kill two birds with one stone? We been riding fo' a long time, and my stomach is running on empty. That sign says there's a restaurant 'bout a mile up the road, you can wash that sweet ass of yours and we can get our grub on too."

Leaving the freeway at the next exit, Sharon pulls onto the restaurant parking lot and kills the engine. Looking in the rear view mirror, she make's sure that the wig is straight on her head. Satisfied with her appearance, she and Tonya go inside.

"Hey baby, while I go and clean myself up, why don't you find us a seat and order for the both of us?" says Sharon, heading for the bathroom.

Looking over the menu, Tonya is greeted by the waitress whom has a grim, sourpuss look on her face . . . a look that has been put there from hour after hour, day after day of taking countless food orders, and people bitching about this ain't right and that ain't right. Managing a fake smile she asks, "What can I get for you this evening?"

Before she can answer, a tall, scraggly looking white man; about thirty years of age, sitting in the next booth, interrupts her. "What the hell do I have to do to get some service around here?"

"Oh boy," thinks the waitress to herself. "This is going to be one of those nights."

"I'm sorry sir, as soon as I take this lady's order, I'll be right with you."

"Fuck that!" shouts the man, spraying tobacco juice down his chin. "I want some goddamn service and I want it now. That nigger bitch can wait until I get my order . . . now bring your ass on over here."

Embarrassed by the man's attitude, the waitress can only stare at him with her mouth wide open. Before she or Tonya can respond, seated in the next booth is a young, black haired man looking to be in his early twenties, addresses the rude man in a calm, icy voice.

"Mr., this is just a suggestion, so you can take it for what it's worth. The nice lady said that as soon as she takes this nice ladies order, she will be glad to take yours. Now my suggestion is this, have a little patience and let her do her job."

"And just who in the hell do you think you are? You little grease ball looking motherfucker. I said that nigger bitch can wait until I get my order, and by god that's what I mean!"

By this time, all of the commotion has caught the attention of the manager who comes out of the kitchen with a baseball bat in his hand.

Approaching the booth where the man is seated, the manager states in a loud and angry voice, "Sir, we don't care for that kind of rudeness, I think you had better leave."

"I don't believe this shit . . . you being a white man an' all. You going to throw me out and let that nigger bitch stay in here?"

"That's it buster, I tried to be nice about it, but you don't leave me no choice," says the manager, as he reaches down and grabs the man by the front of his shirt and lifts him to his feet. The man's first instinct is to resist. But when he realizes that the manager stands about two feet over him and has the baseball bat in his hand, he rethinks the situation. Grabbing his pitcher of beer from the table, the man turns it up to his mouth and drains it dry. Then turning his eyes towards the room full of patrons that have stopped eating to stare at the scene, he admonishes them.

"What the fuck yawl looking at? It's a sad day when a white man can't sit down and eat without being harassed."

Looking from one to the other, he gives the evil eye to Tonya, the black haired man and the manager. After giving them the fuck-you salute, he puts his backpack on and staggers to the exit.

After giving Tonya an apology and assuring her that her meal is on the house, the manager returns to the kitchen. The young black haired man that had intervened on her behalf reached out his hand and introduced himself. "Hello, I'm sorry if that rude fellow spoiled your evening, some people don't know when to stop drinking and when to keep their mouths shut. Oh, by the way, my name is Juan Garcia at your service!"

Still in shock over what had just happened, Tonya was only vaguely aware of what the man was saying. "Huh, oh yeah. Thanks Mr. Garcia."

"Are you ready to order Miss?" inquires the embarrassed waitress.

In the mist of Tonya placing their order, Sharon comes from the bathroom and slips into the booth besides her. "You mean to tell me that after all this time you're just ordering our food?"

"Yeah baby girl, while you were gon' all kind of drama been going down out here."

With a quizzical tone, Sharon asks.

"What kind of drama?"

"Oh, just some old drunk ass redneck throwing around that ole' nigga shit. You know how they is when they get fucked up off that beer. But don't worry, the manager and Mr. Garcia here put him in check," answered Tonya indicating the black haired man.

Sharon reaches over and shakes the man's outstretched hand.

"Thank you for helping Sir."

"The name is Juan Garcia, and I'm glad I could be of some help. And I do hope you ladies enjoy the rest of your evening."

"This is the kind of shit that we don't need," whispers Sharon as she places her mouth close to Tonya's ear. "Let's get through eating and get the hell out of here."

Chapter 24

The Twi-light Zone

After paying the check, Sharon and Tonya exit the restaurant and start across the dark parking lot toward their car when Tonya notices two men standing between their car and a black Cadillac. One of the men she recognizes as Juan Garcia. The other one was the drunken redneck that had got thrown out of the restaurant. Grabbing Sharon and pulling her down, they crouch behind a parked car so they can see what's going on.

"I ain't going to tell you again, give me your fucking keys!" came the angry voice from the Redneck pointing a hunter's knife at Garcia.

Pushing the remote button on his key chain to unlock the car door, Juan Garcia manages to get inside of his car, but before he can close the door Redneck snatches it open and climbs in on top of him. Bringing his arm up over his head, the girls can see a glint of light as it reflects off of the knife blade before it plunges into Garcia's chest. Pushing Garcia over to the passenger seat, redneck reaches outside of the car and picks up a suitcase that he had placed there . . . started the Cadillac and pulls out of the parking lot.

"Come on, let's get the hell out of here before somebody calls the cops!" screams Sharon as she and Tonya race toward their car. When they reach the car, Sharon notices something that drains all of the strength from her body, she notices that the side window had been broken and that the suitcase that was on the backseat was gone. Immediately her mind did a replay of the image of Redneck picking up the suitcase and putting it in the Cadillac.

"Oh fuck, come on Tonya, we have to catch that son-of-a-bitch."

Tonya, not noticing the broken window, asks, "Why? That shit ain't got nothing to do with us, we better get otta here and look out fo' our own asses."

Jumping in and starting the car, Sharon screams, "That bastard stole your suitcase. He has all of the money and the dope."

Finally what Sharon is saying sinks into her brain. Looking from the broken window to the empty back seat, Tonya lets out with a yell loud enough to be heard three blocks away. "Oh hell naw! That muthafucka ain't gonna get away with my shit . . . get this whip rolling, we gotta catch his ass."

Roaring out of the driveway, Tonya spots the Cadillac about three car lengths in front of them.

"Come on Sharon, catch that fucka," shouts Tonya.

"Take it easy honey, I got everything under control."

"Under control my ass. The bastard is right in front of us, all you gotta do is ram his ass off the road and then we can get my shit. Why you waiting back here?"

"Ram him off the road and maybe kill ourselves in the process! No thanks, there's a better way," replies Sharon.

"What better way?!" screams Tonya at the top of her lungs, "you gon' fuck around and let him get away!"

"He's not going anywhere," answer's Sharon with confidence. "He's playing my game now. This is the kind of thing that I was trained for, he don't have any idea that we are behind him, so I'm certainly not going to wise him up and blow our advantage. All we have to do is keep him in sight and wait until he stops."

"Yeah, all that's well and good but how do you know he's gonna stop? And if he do, how long it's gonna be?"

"My guess is that when he do stop, it's going to be along some dark deserted road" answer's Sharon. "Remember he has a body that he has to get rid of, he can't afford to ride around with it too long. Now how long it's going to be before he stops? I say not long! Remember all that beer that he drank before he left the restaurant? You heard that old joke . . . you don't buy beer, you only rent it . . . well, I'm betting it won't be too long before he has to pay the bill, know what I mean?"

"All right girl, I sure hope you be right," says Tonya feeling a little more at ease after hearing Sharon's plan.

Following the Cadillac at a safe distance, Sharon concentrates on keeping it in sight. After about forty-five minutes, the Cadillac's turn signal comes on indicating that it is leaving the freeway at the next exit.

"See, what did I tell you?" Beamed an excited Sharon. "I told you, sooner or later I knew that he would have to piss, and I knew that he would look for a deserted exit."

After the Cadillac leaves the highway, it turns down a dark service road. Following close behind, Sharon has turned off her headlight's so as not to be seen. In the darkness she had to stay close enough to the Cadillac to use its lights to see where she was going. About a quarter of a mile down the road, the Cadillac pulls over to the side and stops. Straining her eyes to see through the darkness, she can faintly see Redneck get out of the car.

"Okay this is it," whispers Sharon excitedly as her breath comes in short gulps. She can feel the adrenalin pumping through her veins causing her heart to beat wildly.

"It's now or never Tonya, here's what I want you to do. I'm going to work my way around to the front of his car, I want you to count to thirty then I want you to drive your car about ten feet past him and stop . . . make sure you have your lights on. After you stop, get out of the car and ask if he needs any help . . . I'll do the rest."

"Drive past him and get out! Are you crazy? I know that muthafucka gonna recognize me! What if he got a piece and busts a cap in my ass?"

"I'm counting on him recognizing you, that's why I know that even if he has a gun he's not going to shoot you, think about it. He's already pissed at you because of what happened at the restaurant, now here you are all alone on a dark road with nobody to help . . . just a young helpless girl and him. So you tell me, what do you think he's going to have on his mind?"

After Sharon has gotten out the car and disappeared into the darkness, Tonya counts to thirty and starts the car. Turning on the headlights, she drives about what she estimates to be ten feet past the Cadillac and stops. Getting out of her car, she is bathed in the headlights of the Cadillac as she calls out. "Do you need any help?"

Startled by the sudden appearance of the car, Redneck is put at ease as his headlights focus on Tonya. He instantly recognizes her from the restaurant and realizes that with her looking into his headlights, she can't see him plain enough to know who he is.

"My, my, my, there is a god," he thought to himself. "And look what he laid in my lap. This my lucky night, I'm gonna fuck her till she's bowlegged." Having finished pissing, he puts his dick back inside his pants and hollers out, "Yeah darling, I sho' can use some help. It appears that I done run out of gas, do you think you can run me to the gas station to get some?"

"Yeah, I guess I can do that. Come on, I got a gas can in my car. There should be a station around here somewhere," replied Tonya trying to keep her voice from shaking as her stomach is doing flip-flops.

Walking towards Tonya, Redneck is caught unaware as Sharon springs from behind the Cadillac and jams her nine-millimeter into the small of his back. Through clenched teeth she hisses in a deadly voice. "If you so much as move a muscle you're going to have a choice of which asshole you want to shit out of . . . the one you have now, or the new one that this nine is going to make for you."

Sweat instantly began to stream down Redneck's face as he stammers in a cowardly voice. "Who are you? What do yawl want with me? I ain't done nothing to yawl."

"Shut the fuck up!" shouts Sharon. "Tonya, come look in his car and see if your suitcase is in here . . . and you!" said Sharon, indicating Redneck.

"Lay your ass down with your hands locked behind your head. And remember what I said about your new asshole."

Looking in the back seat of the Cadillac, Tonya spots the suitcase and hollers out, "Yeah baby, it's here. I got it . . . let's get the fuck otta here."

As Sharon momentarily turns her head in the direction of Tonya's voice, Redneck jumps up from the ground with his knife in his hand. With a downward swing he directs the blade towards Sharon's chest. But before the blade can reach its target, the nine millimeter coughs to life and bucks in Sharon's hand sending a white hot missile into his stomach. Knocked to the ground by the force of the slug, he is startled by the reality of the pain that it is causing. Gathering his strength, he regains his feet and charges at Sharon only to be met once again by nerve shattering pain as two more chunks of lead penetrates his chest and exits his back taking half of his spine with them leaving his lifeless body to do the dance of death as it crumbles to the ground.

Tonya stands beside the Cadillac holding her suitcase in her hand with her mouth wide open, her whole body is visibly shaking. Sharon breaks her out of her trance by screaming her name. "Tonya . . . Tonya! Come on baby, let's go. We got to get out of here before somebody comes down this road."

Tonya starts for the car when she hears some moaning coming from the Cadillac. With the door open and the inside light on, she can see the body of Juan Garcia. "Hey Sharon, I think this guy is still alive." Reaching into the car and turning his head to face her, she can see his eye lids flutter.

With blood seeping from the corner of his mouth, in a barely audible voice, Juan Garcia pleads, "Please help me."

Coming over to look into the car, Sharon speaks to Tonya in a very angry tone. "Come on Tonya, I don't have time for this shit, in case you don't know it, I just killed that man, and that puts my ass in a whole different category from merely stealing drugs . . . this, they can fry my ass for and I'm not about to stay around here and let that happen, now come on."

Once again in a whisper, Garcia pleads, "Please, you can't just leave me here, please help me."

"Look mister," cried Sharon, "Under ordinary circumstances I wouldn't mind helping you, but I'm in a jam myself and I have to look out for me. I'm sure you can understand that."

"What we gonna do?" asked Tonya on the verge of freaking out. "If we just leave him here, he's gonna die, and he did try to help me in the restaurant."

Before Sharon can answer, Juan Garcia whisper's in a weak voice, "I have a cell phone in my pocket. If you make a call for me you won't regret it. My father is a very important man. If you help me he can make all of your problems go away."

"The only way that your father can help us is if he's the President of the United States," sneered Sharon.

Still whispering Garcia adds, "Compared to my father's power, the President's powers are weak."

"It don't matter who your father is, I don't have time to debate the issue with you. But I'll do that much for you . . . which pocket is your phone in?" Reaching inside of Juan's jacket pocket, Sharon takes his phone and tries to place it in his hand, but he's too weak from the loss of blood to hold it.

"You'll have to dial the number for me," whisper's Juan. After dialing the number that he had given her, she holds the phone to his mouth.

"Who's this?" came the gruff voice from the other end.

"Raul, this is Juan. Let me speak to my father."

A couple of seconds later, a different voice comes through the phone. "Hello son, we're all waiting for you to get here. What time do you think you'll get in?"

With his strength fading, Juan replies, "Father I'm hurt pretty bad. I need someone to come for me."

The tone in Juan's father's voice goes from calm to panic. "What's wrong son? Where are you?"

"I don't know exactly," he mumbled, "I should be somewhere around St. Louis Mo." Before he could say anything else, he lost consciousness.

Sharon hearing the panicky voice screaming from the phone puts it to her ear. "Hello, who's this?"

She hears complete silence and then a cautious voice asks, "Who are you? Where's my son?"

"Look sir, I just happen to be passing by and saw that your son was hurt," lied Sharon, "He asked me to help him make a phone call."

"Hurt, hurt how? Let me talk to Juan!"

"Sir, that's what I'm trying to tell you. Your son is hurt bad, he's been stabbed . . . he's passed out, probably from the loss of blood."

"Is he still alive?" asks the father anxiously.

Reaching down to feel Juan's pulse, Sharon answers, "Yes sir, he's still alive. But you need to come and take him to a hospital."

"Wait a minute lady, you're not going to leave him there by himself are you? You have to give me time to get to wherever you are?"

"Mister, I made the call that's all I can do. Like I told your son I have enough troubles of my own, I can't afford to stay here and wait for no one."

"Miss, I don't know what kind of problems you have, but if you help my son, your problems become my problems. And if your problems are half as serious as you think they are, you are going to need a friend."

"I need to think about this for a minute sir. I just don't know," exclaims Sharon.

"I'm afraid time is something we don't have my friend. If my son is hurt as bad as you say he is, we both need to act quickly. Now tell me precisely where you are."

Trying hard to figure out where they were, she could only guess. "I think that we are about forty miles outside of St. Louis, we're on a side service road off Westbound I-40."

"Okay, here's what I want you to do," came the father's voice that now seemed under control. "The first thing you need to do is stop at a drugstore and get some first aid supplies. Do you know anything about first aid?

Sharon answers in the affirmative, "Yes I do."

"Good. After you get the supplies, find a motel. When you get in the room, call me at this same number and let me know exactly where you are . . . treat my son's wounds and make him comfortable. By that time someone will be there for him."

"Okay mister, I'm going to put my ass on the line and help your son out as best I can. But let me warn you, if this is some kind of a trap to set me up, I guarantee you that your son will be the first one to die."

"I assure you mam this is no trap. My son is the most important thing in my life, so when you help him, you become the second most important person to me."

"Come on Tonya," shouts Sharon after she has hung up the phone. "Help me get him onto the backseat."

With one taking his head and the other taking his feet, they manage to get Juan moved.

"Okay," states Sharon, let's get all our stuff out of your car and put it in the Cadillac. We have to get that body into the trunk. Give me that bottle of hand sanitizer and a rag . . . we need to wipe away every trace of our fingerprints."

After they have done all that's needed to be done, Sharon instructs Tonya to drive her car a couple of miles away from the murder scene while she followed in the Cadillac.

Parking her car and wiping her prints from the wheel before she joins Sharon in the Cadillac, Tonya inquires, "Why you want me to move my car from where it was?"

"Because with all that blood that leaked out of that redneck, it wouldn't be such a good idea to have your car parked right there. That would start an investigation and that we don't need. We need to buy as much time as we can, too much shit has already gone wrong."

After getting the necessary supplies from a drugstore, they check into a motel. Getting a room at the back of the building, they struggle to get Juan into the room because by now he is dead weight. But they manage to get him in and put him on the bed. Taking his jacket and shirt off, they see the deep hole where the knife had been imbedded in his chest.

"He's one lucky ass," says Sharon as she applies peroxide to the wound. "One inch to the left, that knife would have gone straight through his heart." After finish cleaning the wound, she applies an ointment to keep it from infecting.

Checking the last number that was dialed from Juan's phone, she presses redial . . . the phone is answered on the first ring. "Who's this?"

"It's me, Mister Garcia. I've done what you've asked me to do. Do you have a pen to write these directions down?"

Before taking the directions, Mr. Garcia inquires, "How's my son doing? Has he regained consciousness yet?"

"He's drifting in and out. I've done the best that I can, but he's lost a lot of blood . . . he really need to get to a hospital."

"Someone will be there to see that he gets everything that he needs. I thank you for everything that you've done, and remember what I said about you having a friend whenever you need me."

"And I want you to remember what I said about this being a trap."

Chapter 25

New beginnings

"Damn girl," complains Tonya as she nervously pace back and forth across the small motel room. "This waiting shit don' got me nervous as a muthafucka. Maybe we should just get the fuck otta here! How we know this ain't some kind of trap or somethin'?"

Sharon, sitting on the bed applying a fresh gauze bandage to Juan's wound, speaks in a slow uncertain voice. "I don't know Tonya, but I do know one thing, we've gone too far now to turn around. Besides it was you that wanted to help him, so now we don't have any choice but to ride it out."

"Yeah, I said help him . . . like drop him off at the hospital or somethin'. I didn't mean fo' us to put our asses on lock down!" screamed Tonya. "We been waiting here fo' over two hours. Man we gotta go."

"Go where, and how?" yelled Sharon. "Are you forgetting that we don't have a car? Our car is back there with a dead body in it, so we damn sure can't go get it. So that only leaves Juan's car . . . and how long do you think it's going to take his father to find our asses in that? So that don't leave us with many choices do it?"

After venting her frustration, Sharon has a twinge of guilt for yelling at Tonya. After all, she was right about them putting their asses on lock down. She knew that she was betting their freedom on Juan's father being able to help them, and that was betting a lot on someone that she had never heard of.

In a soft soothing tone, she tried to reassure Tonya and herself. "Listen babygirl, I know that things might look a little rough for us right now, but I've got a gut feeling that everything is going to turn out alright. Besides, we knew when we started, that sooner or later we were going to be faced with some problems . . . well, this is one of them. We just have to play it out and see what happens."

The knock at the door sent a chill through the girls, as they looked first at each other, and then at the door. After the second knock, Sharon removed her nine-millimeter from her pocket . . . held it behind her back, and went to the door; asking in a nervous voice. "Who is it?"

"Friends of Juan Garcia," came the polite voice.

With the night chain in place, Sharon cracked the door open just enough to see four of the biggest men that she had ever seen. They were all dressed neatly in business suits and ties. Removing the night chain, Sharon points her gun at them and gives instructions. "Only one of you, the rest of you stay out there until I know what's happening." Keeping her gun trained on him, Sharon allows one of the men to enter the room; quickly closing and locking the door behind him.

"He's over there on the bed!"

As the huge man goes over to look at Juan, Tonya and Sharon stand against the wall with the aim of the nine-millimeter never leaving his head.

After a cursory examination of Juan, the man takes out his cell phone and dials a number. "Yes sir, he seem to be in pretty good shape considering the nature of his wound, they seem to have taken good care of him."

After speaking on the phone for few minutes, the man holds out his phone to Sharon, indicating that someone wanted to speak to her.

"Is this Mr. Garcia?" she asks nervously.

"Yes it is, and I want to thank you again for what you did for my son. Is there anything that I can do for you at this time?"

Thinking about the situation that they were in, Sharon speaks in an inquiring tone, "Well sir, first of all, I would like to explain that what we did for your son . . . we didn't do for something in return . . . but since you're asking, we do find ourselves in kind of a tight spot. For reasons that I can't go into right now, we need to get far away from where we are and we don't have transportation."

"Not a problem, take Juan's car . . . consider it a gift."

"Thank you, that's very kind of you, but that would present another problem. Juan's car is soaked with blood . . . and let's just say that I can't afford to be caught in that kind of situation."

"Uuuuummmm, I see," says Mr. Garcia, "Sight unseen, I'd say your situation might be a little more complicated than I thought, but still not a problem. Remember what I said about you helping my son? Well, I now consider you as my daughter. Tell you what you do. My employees are taking Juan to the airport where I have a private jet waiting to bring him home, I want you to come with them."

"Private jet . . . come home with them?! No disrespect Mr. Garcia, but I don't even know where you are. Plus that, I don't know if your man told you or not, but I'm not alone, I have my partner with me . . . no, I couldn't do that."

"Yes, my man told me about your partner, that's not a problem, now I have two daughters. But before you leave, is there anything that needs cleaning up that might prove to be, how can I say this . . . embarrassing to you at a later date?"

Startled at the question, Sharon's mind races trying to figure out why he would ask her something like that. "What do you mean Mr. Garcia? Why do you ask something like that?"

"Let's just say that I didn't get to be where I am without knowing not only what questions to ask, but also to have the right answers. So in delicate matters I hope you learn to trust me. Now one more time, is there something that needs cleaning up?"

'*What the hell*,' thought Sharon, '*We're knee deep in shit anyway, why not take a bath in it?*' "Well there is one little thing, our car . . . It would be a lot better if it, or its contents are never found."

"Not a problem. Just let my men know where it is and consider it done. Now that that's taken care of, let me speak to my man and I'll see you girls when you get here."

Chapter 26

Homecoming

"What you think he be into Sharon?" ask Tonya in a nervous voice.

She had to pinch herself to make sure that she was not dreaming. Here she was flying on a private jet, when she had never even flown on a commercial plane. If she could've pushed the reality of their situation out of her mind, she could've envisioned herself being a movie star or some kind of celebrity. But no matter how she tried, the truth kept popping up.

Here they were, going to god knows where, to meet god knows who. No, trying not to be nervous was impossible. Her only comfort was the fact that Sharon was sitting there next to her.

"He's got to be into some heavy shit," she continues, "I mean look at this plane. I ain't never been on one befo', but I bet this ain't every day shit. And look at how they taking care of Juan; they got him back there in a bedroom with his own doctor. They giving him blood and everything. Yeah, whoever Poppa big Bucks is, he's one heavy dude."

"Yeah, I agree with you baby, he's definitely a heavy hitter. But I guess we'll have to wait till we get to where ever it is that we're going to find out what's what."

Three hours after the jet had taken off with them aboard, the pilot announced over the intercom that they should fasten their seatbelts and prepare for landing. Looking out of the window, the girls could see a private landing strip that looked to be in the middle of nowhere, within a few minutes the plane glided to a smooth stop. They sat still in their seats as the door to the back bedroom opened. The doctor and two of the huge men that had came to the motel, carried a stretcher holding Juan Garcia, out of the plane and into a waiting ambulance. Still sitting in their seats wondering what they should do . . . their question was answered by the pilot.

"I hope you ladies had a pleasant flight; now if you will come this way, the Limo is waiting to take you to the house, Mr. Garcia will meet you there."

Stepping off the jet, the girls are impressed by the Limo that is waiting for them . . . It's a glistening white Rolls Royce Super Stretch. The chauffeur opens the door to escort them in and offers to take Tonya's suitcase . . . which she refuses to give up.

"No thanks my man, if it's all the same to you, I'll carry this myself."

With a polite smile, the chauffeur apologizes. "But of course madam."

After the girls have gotten settled in the Limo, it drives across the airfield and up a graveled road for about a mile until it comes to a gated driveway. Pushing a button on the dash of the Limo, the gate opens and it travels another quarter of a mile until it comes to a stop in front of a magnificent mansion. With the chauffeur opening the door, the girls step out of the Limo and become awe struck at the sight of the house. It is a three-story building of Spanish design. Its sprawling roofline suggests that it has at least ten thousand square feet of living space. As they drove up, they had noticed the tennis court and horse stables. But what made the mansion stand out more than anything else was the landscape in front of it. There was a pond that stretched the whole length of the house; it was filled with different colors of tropical Catfish . . . the pond itself was fed by several recirculating fountains . . . with the different array of shrubs and flowers that complimented it, It was indeed an impressive sight. As they stand there gawking, their sightseeing is interrupted by a man that comes out the house and heads straight for them with outstretched hands. He is immaculately dressed in a dark blue, pin striped business suit with matching necktie; he stands about six feet, and weight about one hundred and eighty pounds; at sixty two years of age, he seems to be in remarkable condition. He greets them speaking with a heavy Spanish accent. "Ladies . . . Ladies, welcome to my home." He smiles as he put an arm around both girls waist and walks them up the steps to the house.

Snapping his finger, a young boy of about fifteen years of age . . . dressed in an all-white servants uniform, appears from the open door.

"Here my dear, let Hector carry your luggage into the house for you." Indicating the suitcase that Tonya is carrying.

"Thanks my man, but I'd feel better if I hold on to this," replied Tonya.

"Nonsense my dear, I guarantee that whatever you have in there is perfectly safe in my home. Hector . . . take the young lady's luggage up to her room."

Reluctantly, Tonya released her death grip on the suitcase, and watched with mixed feelings as Hector disappeared up the spiral staircase.

"Come ladies, I know that you must be starving, so I've taking the liberty of having my chef prepare you a most delicious meal. It's such a beautiful day, I hope you don't mind if we eat out on the patio."

Following Mr. Garcia through the house to the patio, the girls are at a loss for words. Never in their lives had they seen such lavish furnishings, everything in the mansion spoke of wealth. Reaching the patio, Mr. Garcia pulls each girls chair out for them to set at the food-laden table. There is fresh fruit of every description, along with a large variety of meats, breads, vegetables and beverages.

"Help yourselves ladies, if what you see is not to your liking, let me know and I will have my chef prepare whatever you wish."

At the sight of all the food, Tonya's growling stomach reminded her that it had been awhile since she had eaten.

"Not to our liking, man they don't have this much stuff at Country Buffet."

After Mr. Garcia and the girls had eaten their fill, he snapped his finger and Hector appeared with a box of Cuban Cigars. "I trust you ladies don't mind if I smoke one of these." He smiled as he clipped the end of one of them and lit it.

Blowing smoke into the air, he stated, "Now that we are comfortable, I think this a good time for us to have a little talk and get to know each other. First of all, what are your names . . . it just dawned on me that I don't even know them?"

Both Tonya and Sharon hesitate as they look at each other without answering.

"Ladies let me explain something to you and maybe you'll feel more at ease. My son and I had a nice little talk, he told me about the man that you killed and put in the trunk of your car. That bastard doesn't know it but you did him a favor, if I would have had to find him . . . and believe me, I would have, he would have died a very horrible death. And as for that suitcase of yours, I already know what's in it. My son saw it after the man opened it in the car. But don't worry. As I said before, your possessions are perfectly safe in my home."

The silence on the patio went on for what seemed like an eternity.

Finally Sharon mustered up enough strength to speak. In a cautious tone she asks, "Okay Mr. Garcia, seeing as though you know so much about us. What do you plan on doing with all this information? And farther more, what do you plan on doing with us period?"

Blowing out a puff of smoke from the cigar, Garcia lets out a loud boisterous laugh. "Ha, ha, ha! Forgive me for laughing ladies, I can understand why you're so apprehensive about divulging anything about yourselves, but believe me, you have nothing to fear. Here on my estate you and your secrets are as safe as can be . . . now, do you care to tell me your names?"

After staring at Mr. Garcia for another moment and getting a nod from Tonya, Sharon decides to take a chance.

"My name is Sharon and this my partner . . . Tonya."

"Fine, good, good. Sharon and Tonya. It is indeed my pleasure ladies. Now to answer all of your questions. As I related to you over the phone . . . my son is the most important thing in my life. Without him life would hold no meaning to me. When you went out of your way to save his life, you earned a debt that I can never repay. So as I said before, you ladies are now the second most important things in my life . . . you are my daughters, and all that I have is at your disposal."

"Man, you mean we can stay here in this phat ass crib?" asked Tonya excitedly.

"For as long as you like." Smiled Garcia. "Consider it your home."

"That's very generous Mr. Garcia," interrupted Sharon. "But I'm afraid that we must refuse your kind offer. But we do need transportation! Perhaps we could purchase a car from you?"

"Sharon . . . Sharon, why do you insult me? How could I possibly sell you something that is already yours? I have a couple of dozen vehicles on the estate; choose any one of them with my compliments. But I do wish you would reconsider my offer and stay . . . at lease for a while."

"As much as we would like too, I'm afraid we can't. And we do thank you for the car."

"You're more than welcome. Listen before you ladies leave, Juan has asked to see you. Can you spare a few minutes and talk to him? In the meanwhile, I'll have Hector prepare to show you to the building where we keep the automobiles, feel free to take your choice . . . Oh I'll also have him to bring your luggage down."

Showing the girls to Juan's bedroom, Mr. Garcia motions for them to enter as he backs out into the hallway and close the door behind them.

Walking across the floor of the large room, the girls feet sink into the plush carpet as they gather around the bed. At the head of the bed stands an I.V. pole, laden with a plastic bag of I.V. solution and a bag containing blood, both of which has plastic tubing attached to needles that are inserted into his arm. Juan's eye's open as he feels the presents of them around him. Focusing his vision, he manages a smile.

"Hi girls, I haven't had a chance to thank you. I owe you my life."

"You sho' you should be trying to talk?" asked Tonya.

"It's okay, thanks to you girls I'm going to be alright. The doctor said that in a couple of days I should be as good as new."

"That's good," said Sharon, "We're glad that you're going to be alright. But I was wondering . . . why did that guy stab you?"

"All I can remember is that when I came out of the restaurant, I was going to my car when I saw this man that I recognized from inside, standing beside it. At first I thought he was trying to steal it, then I noticed that the window of the car next to mine had been broken and he had a suitcase in his hand, I asked him about it and he tried to take my keys. We struggled and the next thing I know, I felt a sharp pain in my chest. I guess that's when he stabbed me."

"Yeah, we saw you fighting when we came out of the restaurant, that car that he had broken into was ours. But anyway, I'm glad that you're going to be all right. I think you had better get some rest, it was nice meeting you . . . but now, Tonya and I had better be on our way."

"On your way! On your way where? Didn't my dad tell you that you could stay here?"

"Yes he did," answered Sharon. "And we appreciate his offer. But Tonya and I have a long way to go so we better get started."

Struggling to raise his head, Sharon puts a pillow beneath him. "Hey, you better lay still, stop trying to move around so much," demands Sharon.

Taking a couple of labored breaths, Juan fires questions at her. "Where do you have to go in such a hurry? Where do you have to be?"

Feeling a little uncomfortable by his questioning, Sharon rebels. "I think that's a little too much information, besides why do you care?"

"I'm sorry, I didn't mean for it to sound like I was trying to pry into your business, but I'm not stupid either. The facts speak for themselves . . . you girls are in trouble . . . my father's men reported that when they took care of your car situation, there was no luggage in it. And when you got here, all you have is one suitcase . . . and that's full of money and drugs. Your car had Michigan license plates, so that means that you had traveled a pretty good ways from home. Now tell me, what two women would travel that far from home without tons of luggage? So you see what I'm getting at? You girls are on the run, I don't know from who or what, but you're definitely running from something."

"You think you know too goddamn much," stormed Sharon. "Come on Tonya, let's get out of here."

"Hold on for a minute," shouted Juan with a burst of strength he didn't know he had. "Listen to me Sharon, you need help. And that's all that I'm trying to do . . . I'm trying to help you. Think for a minute, wherever you're planning to go. With all of that dope with you, you're sitting on a time bomb. Either you're going to get busted by the police or somebody's going to kill you for it."

As Juan's harsh words of reality sink into her mind, Sharon's legs go weak as she realizes that he's probably right.

Looking from Juan back to Tonya, she can see that his words has had a profound effect on her too. Tonya can only stand there with a scared look in her eyes as she stammers.

"What you think Sharon?"

With a thousand thoughts running through her head at the same time, Sharon struggles to make a decision.

"And just how do you plan on helping us? You seem to be holding all the cards . . . what can you do for us that we can't do for ourselves?"

"Well for one thing, I can offer you a place for you to rest and have time to think about what you want to do. And right now I think you probably need that more than anything else."

"Uuuummmm, Let me and Tonya talk about it for a minute, come on Tonya, let's go out in the hall and talk. What do you think Tonya? Do you think we should stay for a while?"

"Shit I don't know Sharon, What we got to lose? I mean they already know 'bout all our business, and he sho' be right 'bout one thing, we do need a place to hold up fo' awhile."

"Yeah, he knows about a lot of our business, but not everything. He doesn't that I'm a cop on the run, he don't know that every cop in the United States is looking for my ass. What if they find out and decide to turn our asses in?"

"Sharon, you got us this far on a cop's way of thinking, now let me give you a clue of how a street person thinks. Look at this phat ass crib they live in . . . the jet plane . . . the Limo, I guarantee you they don't work no nine to five gig. And another thing, all that dope and money in my suitcase is grand scale shit to us, but it don't faze them one bit. Now that tells me something, it tells me that they be into some gangsta' shit a lot heavier than we are. So I say hell yeah, let's stay and see what's going on."

Going back into Juan's bedroom, Sharon speaks in a subdued tone. "All right Juan, we'll stay for a little while."

"Wonderful," said Juan, "Just let my father know if there's anything that you need. Right now, I'm going to take your advice and get some rest, I feel kind of tired so I'll see you girls tomorrow."

Chapter 27

Uncharted Territory

Splash . . . goes the water as Tonya's body travels from the diving board and knives through the surface. Reappearing from under it, Tonya uses powerful strokes to swim the length of the pool to where Sharon is relaxing on a poolside lounge chair. Climbing out of the water, she takes a seat beside her.

"Hey wake up sleepy head," she says playfully, pinching her on her thigh. "What you thinking 'bout?"

Raising her arm in a yawn, Sharon answers, "Nothing in particular baby. It's hard to believe that we've been here almost six months . . . and in all this time we've been waited on hand and foot, this place is a paradise."

"You got all that right, I ain't never in all my life even thought about living like this. Man, I could stay here fo' ever."

With a strange glare in her eyes, Sharon looks at Tonya and asks, "Does that thought have anything to do with Juan? I notice how every chance he gets, he tries to put his nose up your ass."

"Oh come on baby." Coos Tonya. "I know you not trying to sound jealous."

"You're still not answering my question Tonya, have you got a thing for Juan?"

"Okay, since you ask . . . I don't know 'bout having no thing fo' him, but if you askin' 'bout if I been thinking 'bout fuckin' him . . . the answer is yes."

Sharon stares at her for a long moment with a hurt look in her eye. With trembling lips, she asks, "But how could you Tonya? You know how much I love you . . . I thought we have something special, I thought that you love me too."

"Sharon, baby, you know that I love you," she replied. "Me thinking 'bout fuckin' Juan ain't got nothin' to do 'bout how I feel 'bout you. I know that you don' swear'ed off dick, and I understand. But you got to understand that I haven't. Sharon, it's been a long time and Juan is 'bout one fine muthafucka. But if I do give him some of this pussy, that's all it is . . . just fuckin."

"But don't I satisfy you?

"Baby, you know you do. I can't explain it . . . you satisfy me completely, but sometimes I just need a little more . . . I need some dick."

"I just don't want to lose you Tonya. You are my life, if I lost you I don't know what I would do."

"That ain't 'bout to happen babygirl. If I sat on a thousand dicks, ain't nobody gon' take yo' place . . . it's you and me fo' ever."

"Hello beautiful ladies," greeted Juan as he approached the pool wearing his swimming trunks.

"Hey Juan," both girls shouted in unison.

"We were just talking about you." Smiled Sharon looking at his chiseled bronzed body. She thought to herself. "Tonya is right about that, he is one fine motherfucker."

"Nothing bad I hope." He smiled.

"What could we possibly find bad to say about you?" asked Sharon.

"Good, in that case I hope you ladies don't mind if I join you for a swim."

"Well actually I've had enough water for today so I think I'll go up to my room and take a nap, but why don't you and Tonya enjoy yourselves?" Sharon gave her an impish smile as she gathered her towel and walked back to the house.

"Come on Juan!" Tonya yelled as she dove into the pool. "Race you to the other end."

Playing around in the water like two kids, Tonya couldn't remember a time when she had felt more free and alive. Racing Juan from one end of the pool to the other, she matched him stroke for stroke as they both reached the wall at the same time. Without thinking, he pulled her close to him in an embrace to congratulate her on her athletic ability.

"Wow Tonya you're great, nobody has ever matched me in swimming before."

In such a close position, she could feel the rock hardness of his body, and as they continued to embrace, she could also feel his dick began to stiffen. As if on cue, they both lean forward with their lips blending together in a long passionate kiss. Tonya's hands travel to the front of his trunks and began to softly stroke his steadily hardening dick, as he in turn slips his fingers beneath her swimsuit and massages the lips of her pussy. Reluctantly pulling apart, he whispers in her ear. "Come on, follow me." He leads her through the lavish mansion to his bedroom.

Sitting on the bed with her standing before him, he takes the top of her bathing suit off. With it being removed, her firm tits with the marble sized nipples spring straight out. Placing one of them in his mouth, he lets his tongue feast on the succulent flesh until it comes into contact with the nipple. Gently nibbling on it, it swells until it becomes rock hard. He removes the nipple from his mouth and lets his tongue travel down to her navel, where he darts it in and out. Laying her down on the bed, he kisses up and down her thighs until her body starts to quiver. His mouth travels to the spot between her legs where he stops and began to blow warm air through the fabric of the swimsuit. As the warmness of his breath penetrates through to her pussy, her clit begins to throb and swell, sending shivers of delight through her entire body. "Oh god that feels so good, Uuuummmm, yes," she moaned with delight.

Abruptly he stopped and stood up. Reaching down he grabbed the bottom of the swimsuit and began to work it down her legs. Removing it, he placed her legs on each side of his head. Lifting her ass into the air, he stabbed his tongue deep inside her pussy, furiously working it in and out. As the friction built up inside of her, Tonya felt herself about to come in record time. "Oh god, oh god, oh shit, uuhh, Uuuummmm, oh shiiiittt."

After her body had stopped quivering, Tonya removed her legs from his neck and instructed him to lie on the bed. Starting at his neck, she rained kisses down his chest to his swim trunks.

"Two can play this game." She smiled as she placed her mouth to his trunks and blew hot air through to his dick. She kept this up until his dick got so hard, she knew she had better stop before he shot his load.

With him lifting his hips, she pulled his trunks off and started kissing his rock hard dick. She let her tongue lick it up and down before taking it into her mouth. As he started to moan under her expert tongue manipulation, she took it out of her mouth just short of him coming. Climbing astride his body, she reached underneath her and placed the rock hard dick to the lips of her pussy and sat down on it. Starting off with a slow back and forth rocking motion, it soon built up to a wild bucking frenzy. All of a sudden, Juan let out with a loud guttural sound. "Aaaaaaaaiiiiieeeeeee."

Feeling the hot eruption of his cum exploding inside of her, it triggered her own release button. "Oh shit, oh shiiiiiiiitttttttt, oooooooohhhhhh god."

Collapsing from the physical draining of their sex act, all they could do was lie there and cling to each other. "Tonya you're everything I'd dreamed you'd be," whispered Juan kissing her neck."

"If you been dreaming 'bout me so much, how come you ain't said nothin' then?"

"Well for one thing, you and Sharon . . . You know!"

"I know what? What 'bout me and Sharon?"

"Okay I'll say it . . . and remember you asked me. I know that you and Sharon are more than just partners. I know that you are lovers."

"What about it?"

"You mean you're not denying it?"

"Why should I deny it, me and Sharon love each other."

"But what would happen if she found out about us? I mean that could cause a problem couldn't it?"

"What kind of problem? She already know we be up here fuckin."

"You mean she don't mind? Man this is wild."

"Like I said Juan, we love each other so she knows I ain't going nowhere. Now the question is; can you handle it? Cause even as much as I like screwing you, if you can't . . . then that is a problem."

"Hey if it's not a problem with you, it not a problem with me. As a matter of fact, why don't we seal the deal with a little bit more?"

"Like I said, I ain't got no problem with that," smiled Tonya.

*****

The presence of someone sitting on the bed wakes Sharon from a light sleep. Realizing that it's Tonya, she pretends to still be sleep as she feels the warmness of Tonya's body sliding under the covers with her.

"Come on honey, you can cut the bullshit, we both know yo' ass ain't hardly sleep."

Not getting a response from her, Tonya snakes her hand down to her pussy and rubs it. Slapping her hand away, Sharon barks, "What are you messing with my shit for? Didn't you get enough from Juan?"

"See there," laughed Tonya. "I knew yo' black ass wasn't sleep."

"It don't make any difference whether I'm sleep or not, you've been gone all the fucking night so what do you care?"

Putting her arms around her and pulling her closer, Tonya says in a soothing voice.

"Now come on baby, you know what that was all about . . . it wasn't nothin' but a fuck."

"Well I hope he fucked you good," pouted Sharon.

"Man, did he! That muthafucka got some good dick and he sho' know how to use it."

"You mean you have the nerve to tell me how good somebody can fuck you?" shouts Sharon, grabbing a pillow and throwing it at her.

Dodging the pillow and grabbing one herself, Tonya swings it at Sharon's head. Before they know it, both girls are laughing as they become engaged in a full force pillow fight. Finally they fall back on the bed laughing and holding each other.

"I swear Tonya, sometimes I don't whether to fuck you or fight you. What am I going to do with you?"

"Well, if you give me my choice, I'd rather you fucked me," giggled Tonya.

"Well what are you waiting for, bring that sweet ass on over here. That is . . . if Juan left enough for me."

Chapter 28

Meeting of the minds

"It's time we do something," states Tonya dangling her foot into the water as she and Sharon sit at pool side.

"Yeah, I guess you're right," agreed Sharon. "The Garcia's have been wonderful to us but it's time to move on. The longer we stay, the riskier it is for us."

"And how risky is that?"

Startled by the sudden intrusion. The girls look up to see Mr. Garcia. "Uuhh, hello Mr. Garcia," stammered both girls, we didn't see you standing there."

"I didn't mean to startle you. Forgive my intrusion. I was just coming down for a swim. But something seems to be bothering you girls, is there anything I could do to help?"

"That's the point sir, you've been more helpful than anyone I've ever known," explained Sharon. "And because of your kindness, we think it's best that we be moving on. For reasons that I can't explain. The longer we stay here, the more risk we might bring to your doorstep and you've been to kind to us for that to happen."

"You mean the risk of me finding out that you're a run-a-way cop wanted in Detroit for stealing drugs . . . or that Tonya is wanted in connection of a double homicide and gang activities?"

Both girls could only stare at him with their mouth's wide open. Sharon's heart began to beat like a trip hammer. The blood rushed to her head so fast she became dizzy. Try as she could, she couldn't make the words that were coming out of her mouth make sense. "Aa-buuuhh, I mean, aa-buuhh, who, I mean how?"

"Calm down Sharon," smiled Mr. Garcia. "It's alright."

"Regaining her composure," Sharon demands.

"How did you find out? And how long have you known?"

Taking a seat on a lounge chair, Garcia starts to explain. "I've known all there is to know about you girls since a couple of days after you got here. As far as how do I know? In my business, I can't afford not to know about everything that is happening around me."

"You mean to tell me as hot as our asses be, you still take a chance on us being around here!" injected Tonya.

"You girls being here have been one of my few pleasures in life. You are the daughter's I never had. As I told you . . . when you saved my son's life you created a debt that I could never repay."

"I don't know what to say, I've never been faced with this kind of situation before. Don't get me wrong, we more than appreciate what you and Juan has done for us, but we can't stay cooped up here forever."

"I can understand what you mean Sharon. But there is a way that you girls can make this your home, and still go and come as you please."

"How you gon' do that?" asked Tonya. "As soon as we leave here, we be hot again, and if we come back, you take a chance of the heat following us."

"New identities . . . I'm sure you girls have heard of plastic surgery."

Both girls look at him and exclaim at the same time. "What!"

"Plastic surgery . . . we could have your whole appearance's changed to the point that no one would ever recognize you. We can also get you new sets of identification . . . Driver License . . . Social Security Card, the works. You can become entirely new people."

"And just how are we going to manage that little miracle?" quizzed Sharon.

"There's a hospital in Mexico City that I have a great relationship with, I can call and arrange everything, by the time you get back everything else will be taken care of . . . what do you think?"

"How long do you think it'll take?" asked Sharon, exited by the prospect of not having to be on the run anymore.

"Off hand, I'd say about three or four months, that'll give you girls plenty of time to heal so that when you come back you won't have any scars. So if you girls are in agreement, I'll start making the arrangements. My pilot will fly you down in the jet and everything that you need will be provided."

A couple of days later, the girls are aboard the private jet, on their way to Mexico City. Holding each other's hand for comfort, Tonya asks, "Are you scared Sharon? I ain't shame to admit I am. I ain't never been in no hospital befo' in my life . . . and you hear all kind of stories 'bout shit happening in foreign countries."

Not wanting to let on that she was feeling some of the same apprehensions, Sharon puts on a brave front.

"There's nothing to be scared about. Mr. Garcia has taken care of everything . . . you better believe he's not going to let anything happen to us. All we have to do is relax. Let these people do their thing, and we come back as brand new bitches."

A S A   P u b l i s h i n g   C o m p a n y

Chapter 29

Heavy Drama

Aboard the jet leaving Mexico City, the last four months seemed like a blur to Sharon and Tonya. Everything had went like clockwork, their surgeries had gone better than expected and their every creature comfort had been taken care of.

There was a sense of excitement about them as they looked out of the planes window and saw the Limo that was waiting to take them to the mansion. As they pulled in the driveway, Juan and Mr. Garcia were waiting to greet them. As they got out of the car, Mr. Garcia asked, "Pardon me, but can I help you ladies, whom do you wish to see?"

At first they were startled by his strange greeting, then the girls burst out laughing as they realize that he is putting them on.

"Welcome home girls, you both look gorgeous."

"What were we befo' . . . chopped liver?" teased Tonya.

"Come on, let's go in the house," said Juan putting his arm around Tonya's waist . . . escorting her up the steps. "Dad has some presents for you girls."

Motioning for them to follow him into his Study, Mr. Garcia takes two large envelopes from his desk and hands one to each girl.

"Go ahead and open them," he beamed with pride. "Inside you'll find everything that you'll need . . . there's new Driver licenses, new Social Security cards, credit cards and even new check books; all in your new names. Sharon, your new name is Crystal Thomas. And Tonya . . . your new name is Darlene Bennett. Now it's very important that you both learn these names and get used to being identified by them and them only . . . as of right now, Sharon and Tonya no longer exist . . . here's to Crystal and Darlene.

And one other thing, this is for you Darlene; your speech could one day prove to be a liability, the way you cut off your words; words like fo' instead of for. I'm bringing in a speech therapist to help you correct that."

"I don't know how to thank you Mr. Garcia, Tonya and I . . . I mean Darlene and I have never had anyone to do so much for us."

"It's the least that a father can do for his daughters. And that's another thing, it's time that you two stopped calling me Mr. Garcia . . . how about Poppa Garcia?" Over whelmed with emotions, both girls wrap their arms around him and openly weep.

"Thank you Poppa Garcia."

"Think nothing of it ladies. I'm sure you must be exhausted from your trip, so I'm going to let you rest. We can talk later, Juan . . . I'll see you a little later."

Crystal, noticing the look that is being passed between Juan and Darlene, leaves little doubt as to what's on their minds.

"Poppa Garcia is right, I think I will go to our room and rest awhile, I'll see you guys later." She smiles as she climbs the spiral staircase.

"Well Darlene, I guess that leaves you and me . . . What do you want to do?"

"Quit bullshitting boy. Get yo' ass up them stairs and get otta them clothes."

*****

Turning over in her sleep, Crystal is jarred awake as her leg comes into contact with Darlene's. Speaking in a sleepy voice, she mumbles. "Damn Tonya, you scared me . . . I wasn't expecting you back tonight. You must've fucked that poor boy to death for you to be back this early." Glancing at the clock on the dresser, it read 5:30 a.m.

"Why are you back so early? You usually don't come crawling back until around noon."

"Juan had to fly out early this morning, he had to go to Sacramento on some business . . . and be careful with that Tonya shit, remember my name is Darlene."

"Yeah you're right, I've got to get used to these new names just like I've got to get used to these new faces. One slip up and all of this won't mean shit if we're recognized."

"Crystal, do you have any Idea what kind of shit Juan and his dad are into?"

"No, and I'm not going to poke my nose into his business trying to find out, and neither are you . . . as good as he's been to us, whatever he's has going on is no concern of ours . . . why do you ask?"

"Oh, I don't know," said Darlene. "When Juan left this morning he was really worried about something."

"Worried about what?"

"He didn't really say too much, he just mentioned something about his father being in a jam."

"Well like I said, we're not going to go poking around in their business, if it's something they want us to know, they'll tell us."

Later that evening, Juan returned just in time to join the girls on the patio for dinner. Taking a seat at the table, he put a couple of spoonful of food on his plate.

"You mean that's all you gon' eat?" asked Darlene. "That ain't enough to keep a bird alive."

"Huh, oh I'm really not that hungry. I don't have much of an appetite," he answered somberly.

"Juan is something wrong?" asked Crystal. "Is there anything we can do to help?"

"That's kind of you to ask, but no." Excusing himself from the table, he mutters, "I must go and speak with my father, you girls enjoy your dinner."

"Damn, he sho' is acting strange, what you think is going on Crystal?"

"I don't know, but something sure is. Let's just wait and see."

The next morning, Juan and Mr. Garcia join the girls at breakfast. Mr. Garcia has a very somber manner about him.

"Girls, I must have a very serious talk with you . . . and the only reason that I'm having this conversation with you is because I consider you as my daughters and I believe that family members should know what's going on in the family.

I'm going to tell you a little story . . . my business interest are many. They include a multitude of things, too many to go into at this time. Some of the things . . . let's just say are not looked upon favorably by law officials. Anyway, there is a family member that I put in a position of trust and now he is willing to betray that trust for his own gain, which puts me in my present dilemma. It has become necessary for me to leave the country. Because of the testimony of this person my freedom is in jeopardy."

Wild eyed, Crystal and Darlene listen intently to his story without interruption.

"What my father is saying," Injects Juan, "Is that you are no longer safe here. After this person goes to court, the government will come down on this place like a ton of bricks."

"Can't something be done?" inquires Crystal. "I mean, can't he be persuaded not to testify? Who is he?"

"Who he is doesn't matter," answers Mr. Garcia, "And as far as persuading him not to testify, there is only one way to make sure of that. Juan and I have discussed it and it would be just about impossible to accomplish that."

"Why would that be so impossible to do?" blurted Crystal without thinking.

"I didn't intend to burden you with the whole sordid affair girls, but if you're interested in knowing, I'll tell you. He's a government official . . . a D.E.A. officer to be exact. He has been an undercover member of the Garcia family for years, now it seems that he has been caught up in a murder. For immunity from prosecution, he has agreed to turn government witness and supply them with evidence on all of my business dealings."

"Can't you just have somebody to take care of him?" asked Crystal.

"If only it was that easy. He would recognize any member of my family, and anybody that he didn't recognize, wouldn't have a chance of getting close enough to him."

"I can do it," said Crystal with a serious look on her face.

The hush around the table was so quiet, you could hear a pin drop . . . then everyone burst out laughing. Mr. Garcia had tears in his eyes as he started to speak.

"Ha, ha, ha! That's very kind of you my dear . . . you wanting to kill the bad ole" man, ha, ha, ha."

In a cold deadly, icy voice, she asks, "Do you want him dead or not?"

Looking at the seriousness on her face, all of the laughter leaves him. "You're serious aren't you?!"

In the same deadly tone, she replies, "If you're serious about wanting him dead, I'm just as serious about doing it."

"Crystal, do you know what you're saying? I just told you that he is a federal cop, so that tells you right there that he's not an easy target. You wouldn't have a chance."

"I think I would have a better chance killing him, than you would of staying free if he testified against you."

"But why would you want to put your life on the line for me," pleaded Garcia.

"Because you gave me this life . . . nobody has ever done anything for me without a hidden agenda. You took Tonya and me, I mean Darlene into your home no questions asked. If not for you, who knows what would have happened to us . . . I want to do this for you."

Fighting to find the right words to stop her from her crazy way of thinking, he asks, "What make you think that you can pull it off? Being an ex-cop is a world of difference between sitting in an evidence room and going up against a well-trained Federal agent."

"I wasn't always sitting in an evidence room. I was a street cop for ten years before I took a desk job . . . but before I became a cop, I was in the Army for six years, and I've had training with every kind of armament there is. I can knock the hair of off a flea's ass at a hundred yards with a handgun. But I have a weapon that him or no other man can match . . . I'm a woman."

Absorbing every word that she is saying, Garcia is impressed. "So my little meek and mild spider has stingers after all. But you haven't heard the whole story yet . . . he's in Detroit."

At the mention of Detroit, Crystal's legs start to shake. Willing strength back into them, she boast, "It doesn't matter where he is, if you want him gone, he's gone."

Staring at her with an unrelenting gaze while rubbing his chin, Mr. Garcia states, "Let me think about this Crystal . . . let me think about it for a while and I'll talk with you some more later. But for now, you ladies enjoy your breakfast. I have some things to attend to . . . Juan, I need to talk to you."

After the men have left the table, Darlene has an incredulous look on her face as she practically screams at her.

"Sharon have you loss yo' goddamn mind?! You sitting here talking 'bout killing somebody, you ain't no goddamn hit man. It's bad enough that he's a Fed . . . but you talking 'bout going back to Detroit to do it. Girl, you got to be otta your fuckin' mind. Plus that, he ain't asked you to do that fo' him, why you be volunteering to do some shit like that?"

"It's called paying some dues Darlene . . . and remember, my name is Crystal, not Sharon."

"I don't care what you call yo' self . . . yo' tombstone gonna read 'dead ho', if you take yo' ass back to Detroit."

"I have to do this Darlene. Mr. Garcia saved our lives and asked nothing from us in return, we owe him."

"Owe him what? We saved his son's life so I say that makes us even."

"Come on baby, get for real. That was an accident and you know it. If that redneck hadn't stole your suitcase, you know damn well we wouldn't have chased him."

"Well maybe . . . but the results was the same. We saved his life and his daddy saved ours . . . maybe and maybe not. How you know we would've got caught?"

"Regardless, I feel like I owe the man and I'm going through with it."

"What 'bout me Sharon? What 'bout me? You say you love me! What am I supposed to do when you get yo' self killed? I love you Sharon, I don't want nothin' to happen to you," pleaded Darlene with tears forming in the corners of her eyes.

"I promise you that won't nothing happen to me, I'm going to be extra careful, I'll be alright."

Later that evening Mr. Garcia and Juan joined the girls at poolside. "Ah my lovely ladies, mind if we join you?"

Taking a seat on a lounge chair, Mr. Garcia addresses Sharon. "Crystal my dear, my son and I have discussed your generous offer at great length and have concluded that your plan might have merit. If successful it would certainly solve a lot of problems for us. But before I can give my approval, we must go over every detail to assure your safety. Under no circumstances could I let you attempt to do something like this unless I feel absolutely positive that you can succeed . . . because anything short of that would certainly mean your death, and that I won't have on my head. Now I'm going to ask you for the last time. Do you feel that you can do it?"

Speaking in a cold serious tone, Crystal states, "I appreciate your concern Poppa Garcia, and contrary to what you're thinking . . . I don't have a death wish. If I didn't think . . . no strike that . . . if I didn't know that I could do it, this conversation would never have come up. If you want him dead . . . he's dead."

With a sigh of resignation, Mr. Garcia replies, "Then on that note, I will question your ability no farther. Now here's what must be done. I will provide you with all available information on him . . . complete physical description . . . where he lives . . . where he hangs out . . . who he hangs out with, everything that I know about him, you'll know. I'll have a complete package on him put together in the next couple of days. I want you to study it religiously. Before you leave here I want you to know him better that he knows himself. And when I feel like you're ready, I want you to go to Detroit and observe him first hand. Most people are creatures of habit. I want you to observe what his habits are and formulate a plan to do the job. After you make a plan, I want you to double-check your plans against his habits to make sure that they haven't changed. In other words, I want everything checked and double-checked again.

One of the most important aspects of your plans must include, and I repeat. They must include a foolproof get away. Taking out the target is only half the job . . . getting away is the most important part. Since your surgery, you are a brand new person. You bare no resemblance to Sharon Morgan, so I feel confident that nobody's going to recognize you so you won't have that to worry about. If you plan this right, you should be in Detroit no more than two or three days, by the fourth day you should be back home safe and sound. Any questions?"

Before Crystal can say anything, Darlene interrupts. "I don't mean no disrespect Poppa Garcia, but don't you got people that's used to doing this kind of thing. I mean, we talking 'bout some heavy weight shit here. Stealing a little dope from the cops is one thing, but my girl here can get her black ass blown away trying some shit like this."

"I'm glad you understand the gravity of this situation Darlene. In answer to your question that you so eloquently asked, yes I have people that usually handle situations of a similar nature . . . but this one is a little different. For one thing, the target is a Federal Agent and even a crooked Federal Agent is highly trained, and the law protects him so he has plenty of backup.

By this person being a member of my family for so many years, he has a lot of friends in the family . . . so I don't know whom I could trust not to tip him off if it was known what I was planning. I'm not going to lie to you. What Crystal has offered to do will undoubtedly be the most dangerous thing she has ever done in her life. But she has convinced me that with the right planning, her chances at success are excellent otherwise I wouldn't consent to it."

"All that's well and good," says Darlene as tears began to stream down her cheeks. "But if something goes wrong, she's dead! Uh uh, I'm going with her, she's going to need some help!"

"No Darlene, I've got to do this by myself!" shouts Crystal trying to hold back tears of her own in reaction to Darlene's. "I'm not dissing you baby, but you'll only get in the way; I'm going to have enough to worry about without having to worry about you. Believe me, I can do this better by myself."

Chapter 30

Down to business

Exiting the Detroit City Airport, Crystal has just completed the four-hour flight aboard the Garcia's private jet.

Stepping out on Conner's Avenue to hail a taxi, she realizes that in the year that she has been gone, Detroit has under gone very little change. As the taxi makes its way down Gratiot Avenue, she looks out of the window to view the same old sights . . . the same old people doing the same old things.

After the taxi has dropped her off at the hotel that she has chosen and she has checked into her room, she relaxes on the bed. Opening a large brown envelope, she shakes out the contents. Written across the top off an 8x10 color photograph is the name: 'Manuel Lopez'. As she studies it for what seems like the hundredth time, she makes sure that she takes in every detail of it.

Satisfied that she could recognize him in a crowd at a single glance, she moves on to a written report on him. Smiling to herself, she had to give Poppa Garcia credit. He had supplied her with enough intelligence on him to have multiple options of doing the job. A couple of things in the report gave her some clues as to the safest way to handle the situation. It seemed that Lopez loved to attend live plays on the opening night and afterwards, have dinner in a particular diner located in Mexican Town.

He fancied himself as quite a ladies man, so he didn't have a special girlfriend, which explained why he always went out alone. His thing was to meet a different woman every time he went out. And whoever that happened to be, that was his bedmate for the night. Another thing that caught Crystal's eye was the fact that Lopez had a fondness for black women.

Scanning through the newspaper that she had picked up on her way to her room, she searched through the entertainment section. Her efforts paid off, there was a live play and this was opening tonight. It wasn't a sure bet, but with it being opening night, she had a hunch that he might be there. The play started at 6:00 p.m. After calling the theater to make sure they still had seats available, she had just enough time to shower and dress to get there on time.

Catching a taxi to the theater, Crystal is resplendently dressed in a snow-white pants suit with a low cut neckline. She has a black mink cape draped around her shoulders to accent her black strapless heels.

After purchasing her ticket, she takes a seat in the lounge; making sure that she is seated where she can observe everyone that comes into the theatre. Her heart skips a beat as a waiter comes to her table to take her order, she feels faint when she realizes that the waiter is a cop that is moonlighting on a second job; she had worked with him for years.

"Do you care for a cocktail Miss?"

Her stomach felt like she was going to throw up as she forced herself to look him eye to eye and answered, "Yes thank you, I'll have a Pina Colada."

Without the slightest sign of recognition, the waiter takes her order and goes to fill it. With the comfort and confidence that she wouldn't be recognized, she enjoyed her drink as she kept surveillance on who entered the theater.

The crowd grew larger as it got closer to curtain time, finally the attendants started collecting tickets and admitting the patrons into the auditorium. After the crowd has gone inside to take their seats, she is left alone in the lounge; there has been no sign of Lopez. So as not to arouse any suspicion, she goes outside and stand near the entrance. Glancing at her watch, she sees that the play has been going on about half an hour and still no Lopez.

"Well, count one for the rabbit," she says to herself. "But there's always tomorrow."

Early the next morning, Crystal takes a taxi to the airport's rental car office and rents a nondescript plain sedan. According to her intelligence report, Lopez should be checking in at the Federal Courthouse about this time, so that's where she headed.

Leaving the Lodge Freeway at the Lafayette exit, she travel's eastbound to a parking lot that is directly across from the courthouse. Parking in a spot that gives her a clear view of whoever enters, she shuts her motor off and waits. Many people come and go, but finally after about an hour, her pulse began to quicken . . . going up the steps into the courthouse was Captain Manuel Lopez. Quickly she leaves her car and goes into the building. Clearing the security checkpoint, she sees Lopez going into the snack shop. Willing herself to think fast, she goes in behind him as he stands in line to pay for his coffee. Tapping him on his shoulder, she asks, "Excuse me sir, do you have change for a five? I want to get a paper from the machine."

Turning around to see who was asking, Lopez looks at Crystal's smiling face and the dog instantly comes out of him. Reaching into his pocket and extracting a roll of bills, he replies, "I sure do. For somebody as cute as you are, I have anything you need." He flirted. "Do you work here?"

"Not yet, I'm just here for an interview," lied Crystal.

"Thanks for the change, I'd better get my paper and get upstairs . . . I don't want to be late."

"Naw, that wouldn't look good even for someone as fine as you . . . well good luck, I'm looking forward to seeing you around," said Lopez still flirting.

Leaving the courthouse parking lot, Crystal kills the rest of the day driving around Detroit. After spending the last year in Garcia's plush mansion in California; by comparison, Detroit had the look of a third world country, but she couldn't afford to get caught up in nostalgia, she was here to do a job and her life depended upon her staying tunnel focused. After enjoying a light snack, she went back to the hotel room and using her cell phone, she called Darlene.

Darlene's voice got excited when she recognized Crystal's.

"Hey Baby, you all right? I been worried to death 'bout you. You take care that business yet?"

"Hold on honey slow down, I'm okay. No I haven't . . . probably tonight, I think I should have everything taken care of by tonight . . . I should be home by tomorrow."

"All right Crystal I'll be waiting for you, and listen . . . don't you go taking no stupid ass chances. If things don't look right, fuck that shit. Get yo' ass otta there and come home."

"I hear you baby. I'm going to take a quick nap cause I think I'm going to have a busy night tonight. I'll see you tomorrow."

*****

Getting up from her nap, Crystal showers and adorns a drop dead gorgeous, full length gold colored evening gown that has a slit on the side that stops just shy of her hip. With every step she takes, the slit kicks open to reveal her beautiful shapely leg from hip to toe. Adjusting the long golden blond wig on her head, she is pleased with the image that stares back at her from the mirror. Checking herself one final time, she leaves for the theater.

Arriving in plenty of time, once again after purchasing a ticket, she takes up her position in the lounge where she can observe anyone that comes in.

After nursing a Pina Colada for about half an hour, her patience pays off, she has to blink twice to make sure that her eyes are not deceiving her . . . approaching the ticket counter was none other than Captain Manuel Lopez.

With it being too early to be admitted into the auditorium, Lopez comes into the lounge to have a drink and wait. As his glaze searches the lounge for an empty table, he notices Crystal sitting all alone. The way that she is sitting, the evening gown has fallen away from her lap to showcase her thigh and leg. Finally looking up to her face, there was something familiar about her. After a second he remembers. Walking over to her table, he smiles and says, "Excuse me Miss, but didn't we meet earlier today at the courthouse?"

Faking surprise, Crystal looks up pretending not to recognize him. "I'm sorry! Who are you?"

"I'm your knight in shining armor, you know, the guy that came to your rescue with the change for five dollars."

"Oh forgive me, I'm afraid I have such a short memory, how are you?"

"All's forgiven, may I sit down? . . . Wait a minute, now it's my turn to apologize. I should have asked if you are with someone?"

"No, I came alone. Please . . . have a seat." Crystal purred in her sexiest tone."

Taking a seat at the table, he offers. "May I buy you another drink? I'm sorry, I didn't get your name."

"That's kind of you, but it's pretty close to curtain time, I probably wouldn't have time to drink it . . . and my name is Crystal."

"Yeah, you're probably right. I didn't realize it was that close," he said looking at his watch. "But what about after the show? As a matter of fact . . . how about dinner and drinks?"

"Thanks for asking, but I don't think so. I don't know if I got that job today or not, so I have to get up pretty early in the morning and start looking again. They are starting to seat people now, so I think I'd better be going in.

Refusing to give up, Lopez pleaded his case. "That's even more reason why you should have dinner with me. If you didn't get the job, you should be saving your money. After all, you still have to eat. Have you had dinner yet?"

Hesitating with her answer, Crystal replies, "No I haven't had dinner yet but I don't know. I mean . . . I don't even know your name."

Jumping at the momentary opening, he quickly answers as he holds out his hand. "That part is easy, my name is Manuel Lopez."

"It's nice to meet you Mr. Lopez, but I still don't know . . ."

"Manuel . . . call me Manuel. Okay I'll tell you what, go on in and enjoy the play and think about it. After it's over, meet me back here and we'll see what happens. Fair enough?"

Getting up from the table, Crystal answers, "Fair enough!"

Chapter 31

Dead of the night

Pushing through the exiting crowd, Crystal feels someone tapping her on the shoulder.

"Let's go to the lounge, it's not quite as crowded in there," urged Lopez.

Taking her arm, he guided her to a table and took a seat. "Now, that's a lot better . . . with everybody trying to get out of here at the same time, it a wonder that they don't trample each other to death. Two questions for you . . . number one . . . how did you like the play? Number two . . . where would you like to have dinner?"

"Oh I enjoyed the play very much, I always love Tyler Perry's plays, I haven't missed one yet." Crystal added in a soft tone. "Now as far as your second question, you seem to be very sure of yourself . . . I haven't said that I would have dinner with you."

Taking her hand and placing it to his lips, he gently kissed it before answering.

"But I know you will . . . after all, how could a lady as beautiful as yourself turn down the request of a starving man."

Giggling, Crystal answers coyly. "Man you sure have a way with words . . . you're something else."

Smiling, Lopez takes charge. "If you like Mexican food, I know this place in Mexican Town that serve the best food in the world."

"I love Mexican food but . . . "

"No buts about it," injected Lopez. "It's settled, Mexican food it is. Come on lets go before I starve to death."

"But what about my car? It's parked on the lot."

"Don't worry about it, it'll be fine right where it is. After dinner I'll bring you back to get it."

"You have an answer for everything don't you. Awh what the hell . . . all right lets go to dinner. After all, I wouldn't want your death to be on my conscience now would I," smiled Crystal.

*****

"You sure were telling the truth about the food," said Crystal as she finished the last of her Tostado Salad. I have to admit, this is the best Mexican food that I've ever eaten."

"See, I told you. I knew you would like It." beamed Lopez with pride as if he had prepared it himself. "Here, let me pour you some more Sangria."

"No thank you Manuel that wine is pretty potent. I think my head has already began to spin a little."

"Nonsense pretty lady, good Mexican Food always calls for plenty of Sangria." Smiles Lopez filling her glass to the rim. "Drink up, live a little."

After finishing off the pitcher of powerful wine, Lopez detects a difference in Crystal's voice . . . it has taken on a slurred quality.

"Manuel, I've had a wonderful time. I thank you for a great dinner and for introducing me to this wonderful wine . . . what did you call it again?"

"Sangria, it's called Sangria . . . and you're more than welcome."

After paying the check, Lopez escorts Crystal to his car. Noticing that she is walking unsteady, he puts his arm around her waist. Once in the car, he starts out with light conversation. Keeping one eye on the road and the other on her, he smiles to himself as he notices her head slightly bobbing from the effect of the wine.

"Crystal, I don't think you should drive home tonight. I'll tell you what! I have a spare bedroom at my house; you're perfectly welcome to use it. You can get a good night's sleep and tomorrow morning, I'll take you to get your car. What do you think?"

Not hearing any response, Lopez turns to Crystal and sees that she has fallen asleep. "Perfect," he says to himself.

Driving the short distance to his home, he pulls the car into his garage and pushes a button for the door to go down. Grabbing Crystal by the arm, he half walks and half pulls her into the house. The act of walking dulls some of the effect of the wine from Crystal's brain.

"What's going on here, where am I?"

"You're perfectly safe," assured Lopez. "Looks like the Sangria was a little too strong for you. You're in no shape to drive home so I brought you to my home where I know you'll be safe, I'll drive you home in the morning."

"Oh no, I can't do that!" screamed Crystal, "You have to take me to my car right now!"

"Okay I'll tell you what. Let me make us a cup of coffee, then after you feel better, we'll leave . . . how does that sound?"

"That's sweet of you Manuel, but I think I should be going now."

As if someone had clicked on a switch, Lopez's whole demeanor changed. "Sweet my ass!" He hollered at the top of his voice. "Bitch I've been sweet to you all night, you're just like all of the other whores I've been out with. It's all right for a man to wine and dine your ass, but when he wants a little thank you . . . that's when the bullshit starts. But not tonight, no sir, not tonight . . . and give me that goddamn purse, you might be crazy enough to have a gun, I don't put nothing past you bitches."

Snatching the purse from her hand, he turns it upside down with the contents spilling on the floor. Crystal's heart skips a beat as the small twenty-five caliber automatic handgun spills out with them. Quickly grabbing it from the floor, Lopez waves it over his head like a crazy man.

"And just what in the fuck do you think you were going to do with this. Maybe you were planning to pop a cap in ole' Lopez's ass huh? I told you I don't trust you black bitches no farther than I can see you . . . and this is why."

Screaming as loud as she can, Crystal asks, "What are you talking about?! Sure I have a gun . . . I carry it for my own protection, but what does that have to do with you? I don't even know you."

Still waving the gun, Lopez shouts, "It don't matter what it was for, it's mine now! All I wanted was to have a little fun with you and then I would've taken you back to your car. But you came here with a gun so that changes things . . . Oh I'm still going to fuck the shit out of you, but now I'm going to do it the rough way."

Grabbing Crystal by the front of her evening gown, he slams her with all of his strength against the wall. "If you have the nerve to have a gun, what else have you got hidden on you? The only way I can be sure is for you to strip . . . so get started."

"Why are you doing this?" begged Crystal. Why don't you just let me go? I promise I won't tell anybody."

Lopez starts to laugh out loud. "Ha, ha, ha. You won't tell anybody. Ha, ha, ha, that's pretty good. Bitch let me let you in on a little surprise. I'm a cop . . . a federal cop at that. Now you put that together with the fact that we were seen having dinner together and left the restaurant together, you know what that means? . . . consensual sex. So who's going to take your word over mine?" To emphasize his point, he slaps her hard across the face. "So strip."

With a tear glistening in her eye, Crystal undoes the zipper on her gown and let it fall to the floor. Standing there in her panties, she stares defiantly at him.

Standing back to admire her body, Lopez barks, "When I said strip, I mean everything. You might be hiding something in your underwear. Ha, ha, ha." Curling his lips into a sneer, he repeats his order. "Don't let me have to tell you again bitch . . . strip . . . draws and all."

Reaching behind her back, Crystal undo the snaps on her bra and let it fall . . . peeling her panties down her legs, she steps out of them and leaves them laying at her feet.

Sweat began to form on Lopez's forehead as he stares at crystals naked body. "Well kiss my ass if you're not the finest black bitch I've ever seen. Bring your black ass over here and lay on this couch."

Walking as if she were going to an execution, Crystal comes to the couch and lies down. Pulling her legs apart to expose her pussy, Lopez opens his pants, pulls out his dick and shoves it into her . . . he pumps two times and cums. "Damn that's some good pussy. The night is still young baby, come on in the bedroom, we're going to have a lot of fun before morning."

"All right Manuel, I'll do whatever you say . . . but first, can I have a drink?" asks Crystal in a subdued tone.

"Now you're talking right Crystal. Sure you can have a drink. In fact I'll have one with you. Is rum and coke all right?"

Making her stand naked at the door, Lopez goes into the kitchen and prepares two drinks. With her following him, he leads her into his bedroom and places the drinks on his nightstand.

"Go in the bathroom and take a shower. Don't even think about closing the door, leave it open so I can watch you from here," he demands. "But wait, before you go I want you to suck this dried cum off my dick, it's starting to itch."

"What? Come on Manuel, you don't have to do this to me," Crystal pleaded. "I've already said that I would do whatever you wanted me to."

Taking his hand, he slaps her across the face so hard that her bottom lip burst wide-open spewing blood all over him. Grabbing her head, he force's his dick into her bloody mouth. "Bitch, when I tell you to do something goddamn it, do it!"

After taking a shower and cleaning the blood from her mouth as best she can, Crystal exits the adjoining bathroom . . . comes back into the bedroom and sits on the bed.

"Look at all this blood that you got on me, now I've got to take a shower too," shouts Lopez. "I'll be right back and you damn sure better be ready when I do. Oh by the way, don't even think about trying to leave. I'll be watching your ass like a hawk."

As soon as he steps into the bathroom, Crystal digs her fingers under her wig and takes out a small glass vial. Opening it, she pours the contents into one of the glasses of liquor on the nightstand and stirs it until it dissolves. Putting the top back on, she puts the vial back under her wig.

"Okay bitch, let's get this party started," says a smug Lopez, dripping wet from the shower. "Give me one of those drinks so I can get my motor running."

Picking up one of the drinks, she passes it to him. Just as it touches his lips he stops.

"Oh no, I'm not that stupid. You've probably spit in this one . . . give me the other one."

Giving him the other one, crystal sits the first one back down.

"You asked for a drink, now pick it back up and drink it!" yelled Lopez. "Unless there's something wrong with it."

"What could be wrong with it?" cried Crystal. "You're the one that fixed them."

"Don't get smart with me black ass bitch. Drink the goddamn drink or I'm going to force it down your throat."

Not having any choice, Crystal places the glass to her lips and sips the drink. "The liquor burns my lip," she complained.

"Would it feel better if my foot burned your ass?" warned Lopez.

Left with no alternative, Crystal puts the glass to her lips, turns it up and drains it.

"That's better," smiles Lopez doing the same to his glass. "Now let's have some fun. This is your lucky day, I don't usually eat black bitch's pussy but in your case I'm going to make an exception. You're so damn fine that if I didn't taste it, by tomorrow I'd want to kick myself in the ass. So come on I'm going to give you the thrill of your lifetime."

Crystal lies there as Lopez darts his tongue in and out of her pussy. The longer he stays at it, the stronger the hatred builds up inside her. The rage that was building up inside her was more powerful than any sexual feeling that she could've ever gotten from having her pussy eaten . . . not to mention that he couldn't eat it worth a damn anyway.

After enduring his sloppy attempt at eating her pussy, Crystal is aware that his attempts are getting weaker and weaker until he stops altogether and sits up on the bed.

She watches in silence as Lopez began to clutch his chest and began to sweat profusely.

"What's wrong lover?" Crystal asks with a knowing smile beginning to form on her swollen lips. She could hear the panic in his voice as he mumbles.

"I don't know! I can hardly catch my breath, I can't breathe."

Getting up from the bed and standing on the other side of the room, Crystal began to smirk. "Sure you can. A big strong raping motherfucker like you! Now how in the world could anything stop you from finishing your job? . . . come on lover, finish giving me the thrill of my life."

It dawns on Lopez that whatever is wrong with him, Crystal is somehow responsible for it. "You rotten black ass bitch!" shouts Lopez still holding his chest trying to keep his wildly beating heart from jumping out. "What have you done to me?"

"Since you asked, let me tell you a little story," says Crystal, now with a full smile on her face. "I know that you've probably seen those erectile dysfunction commercials where they tell you that if you're taking any kind of nitrate, not to take the little blue pill. Well, my bad for not letting you read the label. But because you've been so nice to me, I thought I'd do something nice for you. I put a highly concentrated solution of Nitroglycerin and Viagra in your drink and according to my understanding, in about another two minutes your heart should be beating so fast that your blood pressure will drop to nothing, causing your rotten stinking ass to go to hell so you can be with your daddy . . . the devil."

Through the fear and panic, Lopez asks, "How could you spike my drink? I made you trade with me."

"Yeah, just like I figured you would do. That's why I tried to give you the good one. I knew you wouldn't trust me so I put the shit in the one that I was going to keep for myself . . . boy you're smart."

Trying to get up from the bed, Lopez discovers that his legs are too weak to support him. The more he struggled, the weaker he became.

"Crystal help me, call an ambulance for me, I'll make it right by you, I swear it, you can't just let me die, not over a little rough sex play . . . please."

"You didn't let me finish telling you my story, you're not going to die because of what you did to me. This is a hit . . . you're going to die because Mr. Garcia wants you dead."

At the mention of Garcia's name, Lopez's eyes become wide with naked fear. "Mr. Garcia! How do you know Mr. Garcia? What does he have to do with it?"

"Enough talk," said Crystal sticking her finger in her pussy and putting it to his nose. "The last thing I want for your miserable ass to remember is the name Garcia and the smell of my pussy."

After watching Lopez's breathing stop. Crystal waits an extra ten minutes before she relaxes. Checking the body and feeling for a pulse and not finding any, she breathes a sigh of relief. Getting dressed, she spends the next thirty minutes wiping her prints from anywhere she might have touched. She washes both glasses and put them in the cabinet, satisfied that nothing would reveal that she was there, she gets Lopez's keys from where she had seen him put them, backs his car from the garage, lets the door down and drives away.

Dialing a number on her cell phone, she asks the pilot how long would it take for him to be ready for takeoff?

"Good evening Miss. Crystal," came the pilot's sleepy voice. "I just have to get dressed and go to the airport and file a flight plan. The plane is already fueled . . . so I'd say about three hours."

"That would be great, I'll see you then," said Crystal hanging up her phone.

Parking Lopez's car about two blocks from the theater where she had left her car, she quickly covers the distance, gets her car and drives back to her hotel. With over three hours to kill, she had plenty of time to shower and change clothes. Three hours later, she had turned in her rental car and was aboard the Garcia Jet heading home.

Chapter 32

No place like home

As the private jet lands, Crystal can see that the Limo is there waiting for her, before she can get off the plane the Limo door flies open and Darlene runs to meet her. Being hugged so tight, Crystal had to loosen her hold for fear that one of her ribs would be cracked.

"Damn baby, did you miss me that much? Maybe I should pack up and leave again," teased Crystal.

"Over my dead body. If there is a next time I'll be with you," replied Darlene hugging her again. "How did everything go? Any problems?"

"Wait till we get to the house and I'll tell you all about it. Where's Poppa Garcia and Juan?"

"They be up at the house waiting fo' you, I wanted to meet you by myself . . . they understood."

Walking into the mansion, they are greeted by Hector.

"Welcome home Miss. Crystal. Mr. Garcia will see you in his study," he says escorting them into the room.

"Aahh, so good to see you my dear. I trust everything went well?" inquires Garcia motioning for her to sit down; with Darlene taking a seat beside her. "You must tell me everything that happened, don't leave anything out."

Starting from the time that she first left, Crystal recants everything that had happened.

"Perfect, that's absolutely perfect Crystal. Although I do find great remorse in the fact that you were injured; I'm glad that it was only superficial. Crystal, I can't begin to tell you what an important service that you have done for the family . . . you will be greatly rewarded," smiled Garcia.

"Thank you for the compliment Poppa Garcia, but it's like I told you before, you have been rewarding me and Darlene ever since we've been here. You've given us a new life and we could never thank you enough."

"Never has a father had such loyal daughters, I am indeed a fortunate man. But enough about that . . . this calls for a celebration. When I learned that you were on your way home I had the chef prepare you a delicious breakfast, so I want you to enjoy your meal and then get some rest . . . when you are refreshed, I want to discuss some very important matters with you girls."

"Is something wrong Poppa Garcia?" asked Crystal.

"Not at all," beamed Garcia, "I just want to have a little talk with you, but it will wait until you're rested. Now go and have your breakfast and I'll see you girls later."

Sitting on the patio finishing the gourmet breakfast, Crystal smacks her still slightly swollen lips in appreciation.

"Damn that chef can burn, his cooking is the bomb."

Still chewing on a slice of honey cured ham, Darlene agrees with her. "You right about that, that boy knows his way around a kitchen. Crystal, what you think Poppa Garcia want to talk 'bout?"

"I don't know! Have anything been going on around here since I've been gone?"

"Naw, nothing no more than usual."

"What about you and Juan? Do you think that Poppa Garcia knows that you're fucking that poor boy to death?" asks Crystal with a sly grin on her face. "And since we're on that subject, have you been fucking him since I've been gone."

"I think so . . . and no . . . I think that he knows that me and Juan has been fooling around, he hasn't came right out and said nothin' but I have a hunch that he knows . . . maybe Juan told him, I don't know. And to answer yo' second question . . . No, I haven't gave him any since you been gone. I've been too worried 'bout yo' ass to think about fuckin'. But now that you're back . . . "

"Whoa babygirl, let me stop you before you get to deep. I'm too tired to think about fun and games right now. All my immediate plans call for is for me to take a hot steamy bubble bath and sleep for about forty years."

"That's cool," conceded Darlene, I'll let you rest, and forty years from now I'll still be right here waiting to catch up on what I've been missing."

Later that night, the gentle shaking of the bed wakes Crystal from a sound sleep, reaching over to the nightstand she turns on the lamp and sees Darlene sitting on the edge of the bed. "I'm sorry to wake you honey, But Mr. Garcia asked me if I would."

"It's okay, how long have I been sleep?"

"You went to bed this morning 'bout six o'clock, and its 10:00 p.m. now, so I think you damn near got those forty years in."

Stretching and yawning at the same time she replies, "Yeah, well feel like I could use forty more. Alright, tell Poppa Garcia I'll be down as soon as I get dressed."

Twenty minutes later, Mr. Garcia, Juan, Darlene and Crystal are sitting in his study.

"Please forgive me for disturbing your sleep Crystal, but what I need to discuss with you girls is of paramount importance, it has to do with your future. The reason that timing is so important is because I must go away for a while. I have some business in other countries that I must attend too.

I will be leaving within the hour so it is necessary for me to make sure that everything regarding you girls is taking care of before I leave. You have proven to me that my trust in you has been well placed and that you are capable of taking care of delicate situations. So let me tell you of my plan; first of all, let me properly introduce myself to you, I am United States Senator, Joel Garcia.

Ever since you girls have been here, you have never questioned anything about my private life and for that I commend you. But the fact of the matter is that I have a lot of business dealings that from time to time has problems that can't be taken care of through conventional means . . . such as the one that you just handled . . . And it goes without saying that as a U.S. Senator, these problems can't reflect my involvement at all.

Girls, I want to make you a proposition. I would like to employ you to take care of these problems when they occur. Should you accept my offer you will be given extensive training in the ways of professional assassins. I've already taken the liberty of putting one million dollars apiece in foreign numbered accounts for both of you. If you decide that this is something that you would rather not do, the accounts are yours to keep. If you do decide to accept my offer, then the accounts will be generously added to periodically."

The girls sat there dumbfounded. "Why us? We thought you already have people to do that," asked Darlene.

"Yes we do," answered Garcia. "The people that we have are motivated by money. And anything that is done for money, someone else can always pay a higher price . . . Crystal took care of a problem and money was never mentioned, she did it out of loyalty and that's something that can't be bought, either you have it or you don't."

"Does that mean that we can't stay here anymore? . . . I mean whether we accept it or not," questioned Crystal.

"This will always be your home, but for a while I'd have to say no. The reason being, that job that you just did is going to be investigated. Lopez was the prosecution's only witness against the family, so they're going to try as hard as they can to find something else to hang their hats on, and that means that they're probably going to go through this place with a fine tooth comb and I don't want them to be able to connect you girls with anything concerning me."

"But what do we do for now? Where do we go?" Crystal mumbled sadly.

"Anticipating your answer, I've already made arrangements for you to be flown to Japan where you will receive your training. Everything that you'll need has been taken care of for you."

"How long will we have to be gon'?" asked Darlene.

"Your training will take about two years, after which you will be brought back home . . . also that should be enough time for things here to get back in order."

"Yes Poppa Garcia, we'll do it," Crystal replied. "But I do need to ask you about something else. Uuhhhh . . . our suitcase, you uuh . . . put it away for us and Uuhhhh . . . what do we do about that?"

"Ha, ha, ha!" laughed Garcia. "You don't have to be embarrassed to ask about that. I had your drugs tested and it had been cut so many times that it practically was all mix . . . it was garbage so I got rid of it. But I did pay you for what you thought was the street value for it . . . you'll find that along with the cash that you had, still in your suitcase.

So it's all settled, you girls get a good night's rest and tomorrow you're on your way to Japan. I'll be contacting you in about a month to see how you are doing, in the meantime if you should need anything . . . anything at all, just call and let me know."

A S A   P u b l i s h i n g   C o m p a n y

Chapter 33

Assassins

Pulling the Mercedes Benz into the parking space at the boat marina, Darlene shakes Crystal awake. "Wake up sleepy head we're here. Let's go and get to the boat."

After going to the rental office and renting a twenty-five foot cabin cruiser, the girls unload the car and bring their supplies aboard. With the skill of a navy seaman, they cast off the lines and set a course for ten miles from shore. Taking a nautical map from their baggage, Crystal checks it to make sure that they are exactly where they want to be. Satisfied that they are, she pushes a button and cranks the anchor down.

Changing from their street clothes into bathing suits, they get sandwiches and cold drinks from the basket that they had brought aboard and relax as the calm waves gently rolls the boat from side to side. "This is really some strange shit," exclaimed Darlene. "Five years ago I was a snot nosed 'gangsta hoochie' that had never been outside of Detroit. The largest body of water that I had ever seen was the Detroit River. Hell, I thought that was all the water in the world. Now look at me . . . I'm lounging on a twenty-five foot cabin cruiser on the Pacific Ocean."

"Yeah, well lounging is not what we're here for my love. We have to keep our mind on business, but I do understand where you're coming from baby girl. Four years ago when Poppa Garcia sent us to Japan, I had no Idea what kind of hell we would be put through. I had been put through what I thought was training in the Army, and again for the police force. But I had no idea what training was until that Shaolin Monk got hold of our asses. From the time we got off the plane we were training . . . seven days a week, twelve to sixteen hours a day. We learned how to breathe properly, how and what to eat properly. We are expertly trained in every martial arts weapon ever invented. We have been trained in at least half a dozen hand-to-hand styles of combat and are experts in all kinds of conventional weapons."

"Yeah, all of that shit was hard enough. But the roughest part for me was learning what he called *The Social Graces*, how to act in society; which dinner fork to use at the table, how to wear makeup, how to dress socially acceptable, and how to speak in social society. Man that shit was hard for me to learn," complained Darlene.

"But it was worth it Darlene . . . like you said, look at you now. You can converse with anyone on whatever level you choose. You can blend in with the highest of society's assholes and no one would ever suspect that you were just a ghetto puppy.

Remember that 'hit' that we did right after we came back? You had to pretend to be the daughter of an African Ambassador. Poppa Garcia had arranged for you to be on the guest list at a party that was being thrown for the 'target', a rich diamond smuggler from the African State Department. You mingled with that crowd half of the night until you got a chance to do the 'job' and nobody suspected a thing of you. As a matter of fact, in the two years since we've been back, we've done . . . what has it been now? Eight jobs, and because of our training, every one of them has gone flawless. I remember the first job that I did. You remember . . . that

Lopez hit. If I would have had the training that I have now, I wouldn't have had to take that ass whipping he put on me."

"Don't even remind me of that," snarled Darlene. "Every time I think about what that bastard did to you, I want to dig his ass up and kill him again."

"Well, all of that's in the past now. For the rest of our lives, we won't have to take shit from nobody. We've sat down with Poppa Garcia and explained to him that this is our last job. After this is over, we are on our way to Rio where we're going to live like black queens for the rest of our lives," said Crystal with a dreamy look in her eyes.

"Damn that sounds good. And I'll tell you something else Crystal, don't get me wrong it's been a good run . . . but all of this killing, do it ever bother you?"

"I'm human just like you baby, if I let myself dwell on it, of course it would. But I refuse to do that. The only thing that I want to know about the targets is the information that we need to do the job. And that's all it is to me . . . a job."

"Well anyway I'm glad that this is our last one and I'm glad that Poppa Garcia understand that we want out," chirped Darlene. "Do you think he's going to be alright without us?"

"Sweetheart, Poppa Garcia was doing alright before he met us, so what makes you think he's not going to be after we're gone? Plus that, he knows that if he ever really needs us, we'll be back."

"Yeah . . . but only fo' special jobs," added Darlene.

Glancing at her wristwatch, Crystal states, "We've got about another hour to wait. According to our information, Senator Chavez should be landing on his boat about then."

Taking a pair of electronic binoculars from their case, she focuses them in on a yacht that is anchored a quarter-mile away. "Good, good, his boat is right where it's supposed to be . . . this is going to be a piece of cake."

"Why do you suppose the Senator want to be dropped off by helicopter to his boat?" asked Darlene.

"Some big-wigs are supposed to be having an important meeting with him aboard the yacht and the only way that he can get there in time from where he's at, is to be dropped off by helicopter. Chavez is heading up a new crime commission on organized crime and Poppa Garcia is the focus of his investigation. That's why Poppa Garcia doesn't want this meeting to happen."

"It's a shame that we can't get a little closer to their boat. A quarter-mile is a long way to take a shot . . . even for us," states Darlene.

"Naw love, this is as close as we can get. Even out here, that Yacht is surrounded by security. They have a strict quarter-mile boat free zone to protect it, but we're in luck. There are a couple dozen other boats in our vicinity so that will camouflage our activities and give us cover. But you're right about this being a difficult shot, there's probably about five people in the whole world that can make a shot off of a boat that is bouncing in the water to a target that is swinging from a rope ladder a quarter- mile away . . . fortunately we're two of them . . . no brag, just fact!"

The sound of the helicopter's rotator blades attracted the girl's attention as they looked to the sky. "There he is, right on time," hissed Darlene as her relaxed mood instantly changed to hard cold business.

Opening the picnic basket that they had brought aboard, she extracts a metal case. Opening it she removes her weapon of choice, it was a Whetherby sniper rifle that she assembled piece by piece. After putting it together, she attaches a 500x sniper scope and calculates the settings for the quarter-mile distance. Adjusting the rifle on the tripod, she peers through the scope at the figure that is dangling from the ladder that is hanging from the helicopter to the Yacht. As her finger began to squeeze the trigger, she freezes. "What the fuck . . . ?"

Epilogue

"Come in, Come on in Detective White," said Chief of Police James Hawkins." Getting up from his desk to shake hands with Jasper. "Man, am I proud of you! Look at you. Standing here with your gold shield on your chest, it certainly is a proud day for me."

"Thank you Chief, I owe it all to you. You're the one that talked me into doing this shit," says Jasper with a wink.

"Not me Detective White, you should be thanking yourself, you're the one that made the right choice, I only gave you the opportunity to make it. I remember it like it was only yesterday that you decided to accept my offer and join the Police Department. Not only did you graduate from the academy, you graduated first in your class. In the past five years that you've been a beat cop, you have worked wonders on the streets, working with the gangs. What you and your pal L'll Hammer has done with the G.M.O.C. Club is nothing short of miraculous. The gang activities in Detroit have declined eighty percent and that's amazing."

"Thanks for the compliments Chief, but I have a hunch that you didn't call me to your office just to pat me on the back."

"Ha, ha, ha!" laughed the Chief. "See, you're thinking like a detective already, I like that. No Jasper, the reason that I called you here is something a lot more serious. Remember about four years ago when that Federal Agent, Manuel Lopez came up dead. Well it seems that Lopez was a member of the

Garcia Crime Family. Garcia is a United States Senator and is virtually untouchable . . . that is until Lopez was going to turn states witness against him. Now from what I understand the reason that Lopez was going to rat him out was because of a murder that he was implicated in . . . and that was the murder of Chief Macklin.

The government figured that it was more important to bring down a crime syndicate than to prosecute Lopez for murder. So they made a deal with him. He would hand them Garcia and they would give him immunity from prosecution. But it gets better, it seems that the reason that Lopez killed Macklin in the first place was on orders from Garcia because he had got too close to finding out what was going on between Garcia and Lopez. It seems that half of the drugs that found their way into Detroit was filtered from the Garcia Family through Lopez. So in essence, Lopez was really investigating the disappearance of his own product and apparently Macklin was getting onto him. But he made a mistake. He used his cell phone to call Macklin to set him up for the kill, but he didn't think about the call being traced back to him. Macklin's phone company had records that not only logged the call, but also recorded the conversation, so there was an airtight case on him.

Naturally all of this didn't sit well with Garcia, so he put out a hit on Lopez. Now here's the strange part . . . The night before Lopez got killed, he attended a play in Downtown Detroit. There was a police officer there moonlighting as a waiter. I just happened to be speaking to him the other day and the conversation came up about the missing drugs. He told me that although he had never said anything to anyone about it because they would think that he was nuts, he felt like the person that he served a drink to that night was Officer Sharon Morgan. Not only that, he saw that woman leave the theater with Lopez. He said he couldn't swear to it because the woman didn't look anything like Sharon, but he had worked with her for over five years and there was just something about this woman that stuck in the back of his mind.

Lopez's car was found a couple of blocks from a hotel that was investigated, and there was one woman that had been registered and checked out the night of the murder. A cab driver that was interviewed recalled taking a woman from City Airport and dropping her off at that hotel, the rental car company at the airport had records showing a woman renting a car earlier that morning and returning it early the next morning, all of the identification that she had used turned out to be phony. So that left us at a dead end except for one thing . . . We know that she came in on a private jet, and that jet was owned by Garcia.

Now here's where you come in. There is going to be a meeting tomorrow in California. It's a meeting that is being held by Senator Chavez, the head of the Crime Commission. He is in a meeting with the mayor as we speak and will be flying to California tonight. The mayor has ordered me to accompany the Senator to that meeting to find out what implications Garcia has with the organized crime here in Detroit. So as my way of saying congratulations to you on your becoming a detective, I 'm taking you with me."

"Do you think I'm ready for this kind of thing yet Chief? And where did you say it's being held?"

"Certainly you're ready, as a matter of fact you'll love it, it's being held on a yacht."

The next day, after flying from Detroit, Jasper finds himself along with Chief Hawkins and Senator Chavez hovering in a helicopter over a yacht in the Pacific Ocean.

"I'll tell you what Detective White. You're younger than both of us. You go down first and that way you can help to secure the ladder," says the Chief with a smile.

Climbing down the ladder, Jasper looks out over the ocean and thinks to himself, "This is a view to die for."

www.ingramcontent.com/pod-product-compliance
Lightning Source LLC
Chambersburg PA
CBHW071143260626
47162CB00003B/903